Freeing Ruby

McIntyre Security Protectors Series

Book 3

by

April Wilson

Copyright © 2023 April E. Barnswell/
Wilson Publishing LLC
All rights reserved.

Proofreading by Sue Vaughn Boudreaux, Michelle Fewer, Sherry Fowler-Schafer, Lori Holmes, and Adelle Medhi

Cover by Steamy Designs
Photography by Eric David Battershell
Model: Brandon DaCruz

Published by
April E. Barnswell
Wilson Publishing LLC
P.O. Box 292913
Dayton, OH 45429
www.aprilwilsonauthor.com

ISBN: 9798852101563

No part of this publication may be reproduced, stored in a retrieval system, copied, shared, or transmitted in any form or by any means without the prior written permission of the author. The only exception is brief quotations to be used in book reviews. Please don't steal e-books.

This novel is entirely a work of fiction. All places and locations are used fictitiously. The names of characters and places are figments of the author's imagination, and any resemblance to real people or real places is purely coincidental and unintended.

Books by April Wilson

McIntyre Security Bodyguard Series:
Vulnerable

Fearless

Shane–a novella

Broken

Shattered

Imperfect

Ruined

Hostage

Redeemed

Marry Me–a novella

Snowbound–a novella

Regret

With This Ring–a novella

Collateral Damage

Special Delivery

Vanished

McIntyre Security Bodyguard Series Box Sets:
Box Set 1

Box Set 2

Box Set 3

Box Set 4

McIntyre Security Protectors:
Finding Layla
Damaged Goods
Freeing Ruby

McIntyre Search and Rescue:
Search and Rescue
Lost and Found
Tattered and Torn

Tyler Jamison Novels:
Somebody to Love
Somebody to Hold
Somebody to Cherish

A British Billionaire Romance Series:
Charmed
Captivated

Miscellaneous Books:
Falling for His Bodyguard

* * *

Audiobooks by April Wilson
For links to my audiobooks, please visit my website:
www.aprilwilsonauthor.com/audiobooks

Character List

Main Characters

- Miguel Rodriguez – 30 yrs old, bodyguard at McIntyre Security, Inc.
- Ruby Foster – 24 yrs old, artist, suffers from agoraphobia and paranoia

Supporting Characters

- Shane McIntyre – 37 yrs old, CEO and co-founder of McIntyre Security, Inc.
- Allen Foster – 56 yrs old, Ruby's father
- Edward McCall – 58 yrs old, Ruby's godfather
- Rick Fagan – Ruby's apartment building manager and maintenance supervisor
- Darren Ingles – 32 yrs old, Ruby's neighbor
- Jason Miller – 28 yrs old, Miguel's close friend, also works for McIntyre Security
- Layla Alexander – 22 yrs old, Jason's girlfriend
- Philip Underwood – 24 yrs old, Miguel's close friend, also works for McIntyre Security

1

Ruby

Nighttime is the worst. I'm most vulnerable when I'm asleep, so I keep the lights on in the kitchen and living room of my apartment all night long so that it looks like someone's awake and alert. I keep the TV on all night, too, with the volume turned down low. It gives me some comfort knowing that, while I'm sleeping, my apartment is watching out for me, discouraging intruders. Keeping me safe.

I'm lying in bed watching TikTok, trying to pass time

until I feel sleepy. It's taking me a good long while to fall asleep tonight because I had a bad day.

He was here today.

I heard him outside my apartment door this evening. I heard him tapping on my door and then scraping his nails down the plain wooden barrier that exists between me and the outside world. I could practically feel him staring at me. I didn't bother to look out the peephole because he knows to stay just out of sight.

Pumpkin, my one-year-old orange tabby, jumps up onto the bed and kneads the blanket with his claws a moment before lying down beside me. As usual, he presses up against my body. Even though he purrs loud enough to wake the dead, his nearness is comforting. It means I'm not completely alone in the world. I'm still getting used to living alone. I moved out of my dad's house just two years ago, when I graduated from University of Chicago. I'm still getting the hang of trying to adult on my own.

I already took my melatonin tonight to help me sleep, but my mind still races. A doctor once offered to prescribe me sleeping pills—something far more powerful—but I declined. I don't want to take anything stronger because I'm afraid I won't hear him if he should finally manage to get inside my apartment while I'm asleep.

Day and night, I have to be vigilant.

It's windy tonight—not surprising as they call Chicago *The Windy City*. My old single-pane bedroom window is rattling, which is unnerving. My apartment building was constructed in the 1940s, and it's a bit drafty, especially up here on the second floor. My unit is located along the back of the building, so my windows and wooden balcony overlook the resident parking lot in the rear, as well as the small park beyond. I've never been to the little park, but I often open my window so I can hear the children playing there.

I yawn.

My body is tired, but my mind can't relax.

He could be out there right now, in the hallway, waiting for me to let down my guard. Waiting for his chance to strike.

Pumpkin stretches out beside me. When I reach down to scratch his ears, the purring intensifies. His warm weight feels good against my hip.

He's my little buddy. He's all I've got. I thought about getting a dog once, thinking he would make a good deterrent, but I quickly dismissed the idea because dogs need to go outside to do their business. I don't go outside. *Ever.* I can't very well walk a dog, but I can take care of a cat. I even found a vet who makes house calls for homebound clients.

Homebound. That's me. I haven't stepped foot outside my apartment in two years, not since I moved out of my father's house in Lincoln Park and into a place of my own. My dad told me I was crazy for thinking I could live on my own. Maybe he's right, but it was something I needed to do. Living with him had become too painful.

Thinking about my father is depressing. We had such a good relationship at one time—that was until my mother passed away when I was eight. It was like a switch got flipped—shortly after her death, my father's demeanor toward me changed almost overnight, to the point he openly showed his contempt for me. Even as a child, I could see it—feel it. I wondered even then if he blamed me for my mom's death. For her *murder.*

Today, our relationship is more strained than ever. He thinks I'm imagining the stalker who terrorizes me. He says it's all in my head—that I'm *crazy.* That I'm paranoid.

But I'm not.

He is out there—maybe even right this second—watching and waiting.

Just as I'm about to drift off, I hear a thump when

something heavy strikes my apartment door. Pumpkin flies off the bed and hides underneath. I flinch violently, and now I'm wide awake again, my heart pounding. Adrenaline floods my body, and I find it difficult to breathe.

I pull my blankets up around my neck and roll onto my side, facing away from the bedroom door and clutching the spare pillow beside me for comfort. I don't dare go look. That can wait until morning. Whatever it is, I just hope it doesn't leave a blood stain on the doormat. I've already had to replace three of them.

* * *

The next morning, I'm awakened early by a panic attack. My pulse is hammering because I know I'm going to find something horrible outside my apartment door. I've learned from experience that it's best to take care of these things right away. Otherwise, the smell—and sometimes the mess—gets worse.

After a quick stop in the bathroom to pee, I brush my hair and put it up in a ponytail to keep it safely out of my face during the extraction procedure. I grab a pair of disposable gloves and a heavy duty garbage bag from beneath the sink and head to the living room.

Armed with everything I need, I slowly approach my door. I unlock the first deadbolt, then the second one, and then the third. With the chain lock still in place, I open the door a crack, just enough that I can see outside. Sure enough, there's a plastic grocery bag on my welcome mat. I'm afraid I know what's in it.

I release the chain lock, open the door just enough that I can stick my head out and check the hallways. I don't see anyone, thank goodness. It's still early, and most of my neighbors haven't left for work yet.

I gingerly pick up one of the bag handles and peer inside at what looks like a dead squirrel, flattened, and shriveled up. *Roadkill*. It's been dead a long time, which is good, because that means there won't be any bodily fluids leaking out. At least I hope so.

Kneeling, I grab the grocery bag by one of its handles and carefully lower it into the trash bag. Then I remove my gloves, drop them into the bag, too, and quickly tie a knot. I leave the trash bag on my welcome mat for my neighbor, Darren, to pick up and toss down the trash chute when he leaves for work. His apartment is right next to mine, so he won't miss seeing the bag. He'll know what to do.

Thank goodness for Darren. I don't know what I'd do without him.

Once my door is securely locked, I sink down onto the floor, sitting with my back against the wall. I close my eyes and draw in deep breaths.

Just breathe.

It's okay.

Everything's okay.

I return to the bathroom, strip, and climb into the shower. I need a nice, hot shower after handling roadkill. When I'm done, I towel-dry my hair and let it hang loose to finish drying.

Finally, I can head to the kitchen to put on a pot of coffee. I'm going to need a lot of coffee today—my comfort beverage. Besides having to deal with the gore outside my door, today's the day my godfather, Edward, is bringing a complete stranger to my apartment.

Unlike my father, Edward believes me when I say someone is terrorizing me, and to prove my claims aren't just in my head, he's hired a security company to investigate. This stranger—a guy by the name of Miguel Rodriguez—is coming to stay with me to gather proof of my claims.

The last thing I want is to let a stranger into my apartment, but I really don't have a choice. I need proof. I need a witness.

I'm grateful that someone is willing to help me, but the idea of having a stranger in my apartment is almost more than I can bear. It beats the alternative, though—my stalker continuing to chip away at my sanity and make my life miserable.

I know very little about this guy—Miguel. He works for a company called McIntyre Security, and he's a professional bodyguard. That gives me some comfort. He protects people for a living. Maybe he'll protect *me*. I haven't felt safe for years now—not since my mom was killed. Feeling safe is something I yearn for, but it feels so far out of reach.

While the coffee brews, and my muffin toasts, I open my balcony doors. The early June breeze smells fresh. Sunshine bathes my little wooden balcony which is filled with plants of all sorts—hanging flower baskets and potted trees, ferns, vegetables, and herbs. My second-story balcony is my little bit of heaven. It's as close to the outside world as I dare go. He can't reach me up here.

I really lucked out with this apartment. I have a south-facing view, which means I get direct sunlight all day long. And instead of staring at the back of yet another apartment building, I get to gaze out at a lovely view of a neighborhood park, filled with trees and shrubs and flowers. I get to watch children riding their bikes along the paved paths, parents pushing their children on the swings, people jogging, people walking their dogs. In essence, I get to watch others go about the process of living their lives like they don't have a care in the world. I'm a voyeur of life but never a participant.

I learned at an early age that the world is a dangerous place. There are evil people out there—monsters—who will take what they want without any regard for the lives of the families they destroy. There are those who take innocent lives without hesitation, without warning.

When my coffee is ready, I slather butter and strawberry jam on my toasted English muffin. I settle at the kitchen table with my breakfast and gaze out the balcony doors, across the parking lot, at the little neighborhood park beyond.

As I sip my coffee, I spot one of my neighbors, a blonde woman about my age, twenty-four, named Becky, as she pushes a stroller across the half-empty parking lot to the park. She's a stay-at-home mom. Her son is just two years old. I know this because he was born shortly after I moved in to this apartment.

When they reach the park, Becky heads right for the swing set and buckles her son into one of the toddler swings. As she pushes him, he's all smiles and giggles. He claps his hands with glee. The sight of them together makes my heart ache because that's something I can never have.

The one thing I want more than anything is to have a husband and a child. But that life isn't in my future. It can't be. My rose-colored glasses were shattered a long time ago.

The world is too dangerous to risk it.

After finishing breakfast, I wash my plate and silverware and set them in the drying rack. Then I fill my watering can and water the many plants in my dining room, positioned near the balcony doors so they get plenty of sunlight.

When the indoor plants are taken care of, it's time to go out onto the balcony to water the outdoor plants. I stand at the screen door for a good ten minutes studying the parking lot and making sure there's no one out there to see me. When I'm finally sure the coast is clear, I open the screen door and take a step outside. Pumpkin follows me outside and starts sniffing the outside air. His nose twitches as he takes in the scents around us—car exhaust, sunshine, fresh air, and the plants on my balcony. Sometimes I imagine I can smell the lilacs and the wild roses that grow in the park.

Immediately, my heart starts pounding, but I'm outside only for a minute or so to quickly water my plants. Not a second longer.

As soon as I've watered all the outdoor plants, I shoo Pumpkin back inside and follow closely behind him. I close the screen door and lock it. I test the lock once, twice, to make sure it's secure. I don't think anyone can reach my second-floor balcony, but I can't be too careful. I suppose if he had a ladder, he could.

People out there have a false sense of security because they haven't seen what I've seen. Most of them haven't felt what I've felt or lost what I've lost.

When my mother died, I lost everything.

Thinking about her stirs bittersweet memories. My gaze goes to the photograph of us which hangs on the wall between the balcony door and the kitchen. It was taken at our home, outside on our back patio. My mother loved her flower gardens. I'm sure that's where I got my love of plants. I can still remember the scent of the flowers in our garden, the sound of water splashing in the patio pond, the songs of birds flitting from tree to tree.

This photo of me and my mother is my favorite. I'm wearing a white and blue polka-dot swimsuit, fresh out of the pool, with a colorful beach towel draped over my shoulders. I'm leaning back against her—getting her clothes wet, of course—but she didn't care. No, she's smiling as she leans forward, her arms wrapped around my slender shoulders, kissing the back of my wet hair.

Dad always said that Mom and I were two peas in a pod. We had the same shade of red hair, the same pale complexion, the same freckles scattered across our cheeks and noses. The same blue eyes. She loved calling me her *mini-me*.

And then one day, she was gone—taken from me in an instant—and all the light went out in my life.

My father grew bitter and withdrawn, and shortly after her death he looked at me with utter disdain that gradually morphed into disgust. He blamed me for her death because Mom and I were out shopping for school clothes for me when it happened. Of course it was my fault.

I lose myself in the photo of us together, staring into her crystal-clear blue eyes, so like mine. I was a carbon copy of my mother—I still am. I was indeed her *mini-me*.

I've often wished I could trade my life for hers.

Maybe then my father wouldn't hate me so much.

Mentally, I shake myself. To keep my mind from wandering down a dark path that leads to nothing but pain, I disappear into the spare bedroom, which I turned into my painting studio. In here, I can lose myself in colors and shapes. I busy myself with my latest commission—a tiny portrait of a little white dog with a pink, diamond-studded collar—and try to forget the fact that a complete stranger is going to invade my home today.

2

Miguel

I arrive at the office building fifteen minutes before my early-morning appointment with my boss, Shane McIntyre. I have just enough time to stop by the martial arts studio to say hi to one of my best friends—Liam McIntyre, Shane's youngest brother. Liam and his girlfriend, Jasmine, are teaching a women's self-defense class for new hires. I watch through the glass viewing window as they demonstrate some maneuvers to the students.

Jasmine smiles bigtime as she catches sight of me. She waves, and I return the gesture. It's good to see her looking so happy. Only months ago, she was living on the streets, selling her body just to survive. That is, until she met Liam. Now she's happy and safe and looking forward to a bright future.

Liam catches my gaze and gives me a thumb's up. I wave as I walk away. With five minutes to spare, I take an elevator up to the twentieth floor, where the executive offices are located.

Shane called me late last night and asked me to come meet a new client this morning—well, meet the new client's godfather anyway. The actual client is the man's 24-year-old goddaughter, Ruby Foster.

When I approach Shane's office, the door is partially open, so I peer inside. Shane's seated behind his big mahogany desk, and there's an older, gray-haired gentleman seated across from him. The man's dressed in a brown corduroy jacket, a red plaid shirt, and khaki trousers—he's definitely got a professor vibe to him. This must be the godfather, the guy who's hiring me.

Shane spots me loitering in the doorway and waves me in. "Perfect timing, Miguel. Take a seat."

I suck in a breath before walking in and take the empty

chair next to the client.

Shane leans back in his black leather chair. "Mr. McCall, this is Miguel Rodriguez, the bodyguard I'm assigning to your case. Based on everything you've told me about your goddaughter, I think Miguel is the perfect person to assess her situation."

The man seated beside me smiles as he offers his hand, and we shake. "Nice to meet you, Miguel. Your boss here—" he nods toward Shane "—speaks very highly of you."

"Thank you, sir," I say.

Shane gestures to me. "Edward, why don't you bring Miguel up to date on what you've told me?"

McCall sighs. "Ruby, my goddaughter, lives alone in an apartment in Wicker Park. She's lived there for two years now—and never once has she stepped foot outside her apartment. She suffers from agoraphobia, as well as anxiety and paranoia. She experienced a terrible tragedy when she was young—the poor girl witnessed the murder of her own mother. Despite what happened to her, I think Ruby's doing relatively well all things considered. She completed a university degree in art—online, of course—and got herself an apartment. She'd been living with her father up until then, but sadly their relationship has deteriorated over the years, ever since Helen's—Ruby's mother's—death. Ruby lives a very frugal lifestyle, and she manages to support herself from her work as an artist."

McCall shifts in his chair to face me directly. "Helen Foster was a dear, dear friend of mine. We met at University of Chicago and became inseparable friends. Shortly after she graduated, she married Allen Foster, a financial investment broker here in Chicago. They had one child—Ruby. When Ruby was eight, she and her mother were out shopping in downtown Chicago. As they were returning to their car parked in a public parking garage, they were the victims of a carjacking. Ruby was already buckled into the backseat when Helen was pulled out of the driver's seat. When she fought back, the assailant shot and killed Helen right in front of Ruby. As you can imagine, the poor child was traumatized. The carjacker took off with Ruby in the car. He drove around the city for hours before he finally dropped her off at a convenience store in South Chicago.

"Ruby was never the same after that," McCall says. Frowning, he shakes his head. "She developed a deep-seated belief that the world isn't safe. Honestly, can you blame her? She's coping as best she can, but things have taken a turn for the worse over the past year. She claims someone is terrorizing her—that she has a stalker. Allen—her father—thinks it's all in her head. He's been pressuring her to move back home with him, but Ruby refuses." Edward slumps back in his chair, looking defeated.

"Allen had Ruby in therapy for years when she was younger," he continues. "She's taken a variety of prescription medications over the years, but nothing has helped. Since the carjacking, she did all of her schooling online from home. When she graduated from the university at twenty-two, she moved out on her own. By that time, she'd already built a career for herself as an artist."

Shane nods to me. "Miguel, your assignment is to determine whether or not Miss Foster's claims are valid."

I turn to McCall. "Do you think her claims are valid?"

The man nods. "I believe her. Ruby has her challenges, no doubt, but I've never known her to make things up. If she says someone is stalking her, then I'm inclined to believe her—which is why I'm here."

I nod. "When do I start?"

"Today, if you can," McCall says, looking hopeful. "The sooner we get her some help, the better."

"I'll text you her address," Shane says to me. "I've recommended to Mr. McCall that you stay with Miss Foster in her apartment. Hopefully, we'll soon have an idea as to what's going on."

"I'll need to make a quick stop at my place to pack a bag," I say.

"Why don't you meet Mr. McCall at Ruby's apartment around—" Shane looks to the client "—when? Ten o'clock?"

McCall nods. "Perfect. I'll call Ruby to let her know what time to expect us."

* * *

After a quick trip back to my apartment to pack a bag, I head to the address Shane gave me. When I arrive at an older red-brick apartment building, I drive around back and park in the visitor section. It's not a big building. It looks to be four apartments wide, three floors high, front and back units. Twenty-four units in all. The rear parking lot is pretty well kept. There's no trash lying around or weeds busting through the pavement. Beyond the parking lot is a small neighborhood park.

I sit for a few minutes in my car and study the building. Three floors, wooden balconies for each of the rear units. From what I can see, it looks like a decent place. It might be on the older side, but it looks well kept, at least from the outside.

A moment later, a sleek, black Mercedes pulls into the parking lot and slips into the open space beside me. Edward McCall gets out of his car and waves when he sees me doing the same.

I nod in greeting as I grab my duffle bag. "Mr. McCall."

He chuckles. "Please, call me Edward." He heads for the rear door, and I follow him inside.

The interior is cool, a pleasant contrast to the warm summer air heating up outside. The place smells faintly of disinfectant and lemon-scented floor polish. I follow McCall up the stairs to the second floor, then down a hallway to Apartment 2B.

Edward knocks on the door. When there's no answer, he knocks again. "Ruby?" As we wait for a response, he turns to me and smiles apologetically. "Having a stranger come over is really pushing her outside her comfort zone."

A moment later, a wary and muffled female voice comes through the door. "Yes?"

"Ruby, honey, it's me, Edward. I'm here with Miguel Rodriguez."

She hesitates a moment before saying, "All right." She sounds resigned and far from happy.

When several seconds pass with nothing but silence on the other side of the door, McCall glances at me. "This isn't easy for her," he murmurs. "Please be patient. Take things slowly and work on gaining her trust. She doesn't give it easily." Edward knocks again. "Ruby, it's okay, honey. Please open the door."

I hear the quiet, tell-tale snick of a deadbolt turning. Then another. And another. *Three deadbolts.* The door opens a crack, stopped from opening any farther by a chain lock. The gap is just enough that I can see one pretty blue eye gazing warily through the opening. She glances at her godfather first, then at me. Her eye widens as she scans me from head to toe.

I can only imagine what she's thinking. I'm a big guy, tall, and dark. I know I can come across as intimidating to those who don't know me.

"Hi, Ruby," I say, giving her my most nonthreatening smile. "I'm Miguel. It's nice to meet you."

The door closes abruptly, and then I hear the chain slide free. When the door opens once more, McCall slowly pushes it wide open and motions for me to step inside.

Immediately, my gaze lands on a young woman with long, wavy red hair, a pale complexion, and a light smattering of freckles across her cheeks and the bridge of her nose. Her eyes are clear blue.

My heart slams into my ribs, and I can't look away.

The first word that comes to mind is *otherworldly*. She's stunning and delicate, like an angel or a fairy. Immediately, I find myself having to tamp down anger. If someone is stalking this girl—terrorizing her—I will find him, and I will end him.

3

Miguel

I realize I must be doing a shitty job of concealing my emotions because Ruby takes a sudden step back. She's standing in the middle of a small living room, her arms crossed over her chest, her hands gripping her arms tightly. She's pretty much white-knuckling it. I catch a glimpse of a large, square-cut red gemstone on her ring finger. A *ruby*. It looks old, like an heirloom piece, and immediately I think it must have been her mother's.

As soon as Edward clears the threshold behind me,

Ruby rushes forward to close the door, engage all three deadbolts in quick succession, and slide the chain lock back into place. When she turns to face us, her soft cheeks are splotched with pink. Her eyes are wide as they glance from McCall to me and back again.

In an attempt to stop staring at the girl—and probably scaring her to death—I scan what I can see of the apartment from my current vantage point. It's small and outdated, but clean and uncluttered. The furniture all looks secondhand.

The living room is barely big enough for an old brown corduroy sofa against the back wall and one upholstered armchair. There's an older wooden coffee table in front of the sofa. A matching end table stands between the sofa and chair, holding a brass lamp.

There's a tiny kitchen to my left, with original cabinetry painted white. The kitchen counters are bare and uncluttered. To my right is a hallway that I presume leads to a bedroom or two and a bathroom. The walls are covered with faded wallpaper in a floral print, with small peach-colored flowers on a cream background. The wallpaper reminds me of my grandma's house. The wood floors are dull and scuffed in places, the polyurethane coat having worn off years ago. A few small tapestry rugs are scattered about.

Since Ruby's apartment is located at the rear of the building, there are windows in the kitchen and living room overlooking the back of the building. A sliding glass door leads out to a balcony filled with plants. The dining room is filled with plants, too. I guess if you can't go outside, you bring a little bit of the outside to you.

After a quick visual sweep, I turn my attention back to my new client. She's a little above average height for a woman. She's dressed in a light-colored floral dress with a scooped neckline that reveals delicate collar bones. Over the dress, she's wearing an oversized cream-colored knit sweater. She's not wearing any shoes, just a pair of gray socks. Her red hair hangs past her shoulders.

As for first impressions, she makes me think of Rapunzel—the long-haired princess trapped in a tower. In her own way, this girl is just as trapped as that fairytale character.

I notice a smudge of light blue paint on her cheek, and a closer look at her fingertips reveals more paint stains. I smile, hoping to put her at ease. "I hope we aren't interrupting your work." When she frowns, I gesture to her fingers. "You have paint on your fingers. You must have been working."

"Oh." She glances down at her hands. "Yes. I mean, no, it's fine. I was expecting you."

Ruby skims me once more from head to toe, her gaze wary. Her arms are crossed, and she's gripping her biceps. She's skittish and looks ready to bolt. My heart goes out to her.

Her gaze goes to the duffle bag slung over my shoulder. "Edward told me you'd be staying." Her voice is quiet.

I nod. "That's the plan. I mean, if it's okay with you." I don't offer to shake her hand because I'm sure that's the last thing she'd want. "I'm here to find out who's harassing you."

Her blue eyes narrow. "For how long?"

I shrug. "As long as it takes, I guess. Or until you kick me out. Whichever comes first." I chuckle in an attempt to lighten the mood. "It's totally your call. I want you to feel comfortable."

As she stands there absently rubbing her arms, I get the feeling her oversized sweater is a crutch, mostly there for comfort, like a security blanket. It's certainly not cold in here.

McCall opens his arms wide. "Hey, kiddo, how about a hug?"

As soon as she directs her attention to her godfather,

her expression morphs instantly, revealing a beautiful smile. She steps into his embrace, and he wraps his arms around her and gives her a tight squeeze. He kisses the side of her head. "Let me know if you need anything, sweetheart. I'm just a phone call away, day or night."

She nods. "I will. Thanks, Edward."

"Will you be okay?" he asks her. "I should get back to the office. I've got a client coming in at eleven."

Sighing, she nods. "I'll be fine."

Edward heads for the door and releases the locks. As he opens the door, he looks back to give me an encouraging nod. "Thanks, Miguel. Please keep me posted."

"Will do, sir," I say, giving him a parting salute.

As soon as McCall is out the door, Ruby rushes forward to lock it, her movements clearly well practiced and efficient. Still facing the door—and away from me—she covers her face with both hands and exhales heavily.

As we stand there in awkward silence, I put myself in her shoes and think about how I'd feel in her place. Scared, suspicious, maybe even threatened. Things must have gotten really bad for her if she's willing to let a complete stranger into her sanctuary.

And let's face it, she doesn't know me from Adam. I probably make her nervous as hell. "I'm sorry if my presence makes you uncomfortable."

After dropping her hands and turning to face me, she puts on a brave face. "Please don't apologize. It's Miguel, right?"

I nod.

"I know you're here to help. I trust Edward—he's been looking out for me ever since my mom—" She stops abruptly, as if she said too much. "He's a good friend. Probably my only friend."

"I'm housebroken." I smile in an attempt to lighten the mood. "I clean up after myself, and I promise I don't bite."

I'm rewarded when I see the corners of her lips turn up in a hint of a smile. Her slender shoulders rise as she takes in a deep breath and glances around the room. "I'm so sorry my manners are rusty. I'm not used to having company." Her hands flutter nervously as she gestures around us. "As you can see, it's a pretty small place. There's just what you see here—living room and kitchen—plus two bedrooms and a bathroom down the hall." She frowns. "I turned the spare bedroom into my art studio, so I'm afraid there's only one bedroom."

"That's okay." I motion to the sofa beside us. "I can sleep here, if that's all right."

She eyes me, then the couch. "I doubt you'll fit."

"I've had far worse accommodations, believe me." I smile, so she doesn't take offense. "Really, this will do fine." I set my duffle bag on the floor next to the sofa. "Care to show me around, so I can get the lay of the land?"

"That won't take long." She almost smiles. "The kitchen's there, as you can see."

Between the kitchen and the living room is a small wooden table with four chairs, obviously her dining area. Beyond the glass door is the balcony filled with plants.

She gestures toward the hallway behind us. "The bedrooms and bathroom are this way."

I follow her down the hall, careful not to get too close. She stops at the first door on the left. "This is my bedroom."

I peek inside a small, darkened room. I can barely make out a full-size bed and a couple of nightstands holding lamps. There's a window along the back wall, but it's covered by heavy, dark curtains. I spot a dresser with a mirror opposite the bed, and there's a closet door beside it. Pretty bare bones.

She shows me the bathroom next, which is located directly across the hall from her bedroom. Like the rest of the apartment, it's small and outdated—pink tiled walls, a white porcelain toilet and bathtub, and a gold-framed mirror that hangs over the white vanity and sink. The only thing on the counter is a toothbrush holder with one toothbrush and a tube of toothpaste. There's no window, of course, as it's an interior room.

The last room is on the left. It's her art studio. A large window lets in plenty of light. There are several bookcases filled with tubes and bottles of paint, books, jars filled with paintbrushes, and stacks of small blank canvases. There are probably twenty small paintings hanging on the walls, scattered throughout the room.

There's an old wooden table placed in front of the window. There's a small painting of a little white dog propped on an easel on the table top. Several jars of water and pots of paint are arranged to the right of the painting in progress.

She points to the table. "This is where I work."

"Edward told me you're an artist."

She nods. "I paint miniature custom portraits, mostly people's pets and children. I also paint people's houses."

I walk further into the room to get a better look at the little painting in progress. It's a little white dog wearing a pink collar studded with rhinestones. There's a color photo of an identical dog clipped to the easel. The likeness between the photo and her painting is uncanny. "Wow. You're really good."

She gives me a half-smile. "Thanks."

I have a lot of questions for her about her business, but those can wait. I just got here, and I don't want to overwhelm her.

"So, that's it," she says with a sigh. "That's my apartment, other than the linen closet across the hall."

She looks up to meet my gaze. Since she's barefoot, and I'm six feet tall and wearing boots, I tower over her.

"I'm sorry you got roped into this," she says. "I'm afraid you're going to be bored out of your mind."

"Don't worry about me." I follow her back to the living room. "I'm here because I want to help. And as for me being bored—no chance. I'm good at entertaining myself."

She points to the TV hanging on the wall across from the sofa. "I'm sorry I don't have cable television, but I have Netflix and a few other streaming services. And there's the internet, of course. The password for the wireless router is pumpkin, all lower case."

As soon as she says *pumpkin*, an orange cat peeks out from her bedroom, stares at me, then cautiously walks toward us.

"Speaking of Pumpkin," she says, "here he is."

The cat walks right up to me and brushes against my right shin.

"He likes you." She sounds genuinely surprised. "He's not used to seeing people—just Edward once a week and occasionally my dad."

I lean down and scratch behind the cat's ears. "Animals are supposedly a good judge of character."

Ruby laughs. "I guess that explains why Pumpkin hides whenever my father comes over."

"Speaking of your father—I take it you two aren't on the best of terms. Edward said your relationship is strained."

"He never misses an opportunity to criticize me or tell me I'm crazy. Lately, he's been pressuring me to move back home with him. He thinks I can't manage on my own."

I straighten from petting the cat. "Are you managing okay?"

"Yes. I don't make a lot, but I don't need a lot either. I get by, and thanks to my business, I can pay my own bills. I don't ask anyone for anything." She motions down the hallway behind her. "Speaking of business, I need to finish the dog painting you saw on my worktable. I'm hoping to mail it out at the first of the week. So, if you don't mind—"

"Please, go right ahead. Don't mind me." I motion toward the sofa. "I'll catch up on my reading. It seems I never get time to sit and read, so this is a definite perk."

She smiles. "You're just being nice. If you get hungry or thirsty, help yourself to anything in the kitchen. The pantry and fridge are pretty well stocked." Her gaze darts to the apartment door. "The only thing I ask is that you don't open the door."

"I won't."

"Under any circumstances. Even if someone knocks, don't open the door."

"I understand." I glance around the apartment. "You don't have a security system?"

She shakes her head. "No."

That's the first problem I want to address. "Are there any security cameras in the building? I didn't spot any when I came in."

"No."

I nod, thinking that's going to be a problem, too. I'll talk to the building manager to see about getting permission to place cameras in the hallway so I can see who comes and goes.

"If you'll excuse me," she says as she heads for her art studio. The cat follows.

"Sure. Don't worry about me."

As I watch her walk away, I can't help but admire her strength and courage. Despite all of her challenges, she's still able to support herself and maintain her independence. I glance at her apartment door with three deadbolts and a chain lock. So much fear is keeping her locked inside. She's essentially a prisoner of her own making. She's missing out on so much of what life has to offer—friends, a social life, restaurants, theaters, coffee shops, bookstores. Hell, she's missing out on things as simple as sunshine and fresh air—things the rest of us take for granted.

I'm going to help her, no matter what it takes. The least I can do is restore her sense of safety in her own apartment.

And if someone is terrorizing her, I'm going to put a stop to it.

4

Ruby

There's a stranger in my apartment. No matter how hard I try, I can't stop thinking about it. Yes, Edward hired Miguel, and he vouches for him, but still—Miguel's a complete stranger. A tall, dark, very handsome stranger. Even though he looks so intimidating, he seems like a genuinely nice guy. I like his voice—warm and calm. He gives off a steady, reassuring vibe.

Stop thinking about him and focus on your work.

My current project is a tiny portrait of Tilly, a white Shih-Poo with big, dark eyes and a pink diamond-studded collar. Painting a white dog on a four-inch square off-white canvas is a challenge, but I like challenges. I used a pale bluish-gray background so the dog's white fur would stand out nicely. I like how it's turning out. It's looking pretty good if I do say so myself. I've already sent several progress images to the client, and she's happy with it.

I love painting with acrylics. I love mixing colors and watching how the pigments transform before my eyes. When I was a child, art was my escape. I was always coloring or doodling or painting. Now, it's my career. Not only does it pay the bills, but it gives me something to do. I can easily spend eight or ten hours a day in my art studio and not even realize how much time has passed.

If it weren't for my art keeping me occupied, I'd be staring at the walls and going out of my mind every time I heard the slightest sound.

As I slip into my chair and reach for my paintbrush, Pumpkin curls up in his cat bed at my feet beneath the table. I try my best to forget about my new temporary house guest. As I dip my brush into the paint, all my worries melt away, at least for a little while.

* * *

I've been at work for a good couple of hours when there's a quiet knock on my door. I glance back to see Miguel practically filling the open doorway.

He pats his flat abdomen. "It's one o'clock, and I'm pretty hungry," he says sheepishly. "I took a peek at what's in the fridge. If it's okay with you, I think I'll make myself a sandwich. Would you like one?"

My heart slams against my ribs. "No, thank you," I answer automatically. "I'm fine." No one's fixed a meal for me in years. Not even when I lived with my dad. I always made my own. I'm not comfortable with the idea—it just feels too risky. "You go right ahead and help yourself. There are chips in the pantry and drinks in the fridge. The bread's in the bread box."

"Are you sure you don't want something?" he asks. "It's no trouble, really."

I shake my head. "Thanks, but I'm not hungry."

He nods. "Let me know if you change your mind." And then he heads back down the hallway.

I go back to my painting, but before long I can't concentrate because my stomach is growling. It's been hours since I had breakfast, and now I'm starving. But I couldn't let him make food for me—it's far too intimate. I don't trust easily. It's hard enough having him here in my apartment.

Crap. Now what do I do? I told him I wasn't hungry, so if I go to the kitchen now to get myself something to eat, he'll know I lied to him. I'll just have to keep working and wait until dinner to eat.

I last another half-hour before low blood sugar starts making me feel jittery. I have no choice but to head for the kitchen, passing him as I go. He's seated on the sofa, reading a hardcover book. He glances up at me and smiles. He has such a nice smile.

"How's your work going?" he asks.

"Good. I'm almost done with the painting. I'll let it dry overnight, then varnish it tomorrow." I point to the kitchen. "Just thought I'd get a glass of water." I pour myself a glass and surreptitiously slip a banana from the fruit basket into my sweater pocket. Hopefully this will tide me over until dinner.

I return to my studio, and as I eat my banana, I listen for sounds coming from the other room. I wonder if Miguel's bored. I wonder what he's reading. Fiction? Non-fiction? Either way, a guy who likes to read is, well, sexy.

After a couple of hours, I get up to use the bathroom,

taking the opportunity to peek down the hall to see what he's up to now. I spot him sitting at my table with a laptop open in front of him.

So, what do I know about my new security guard? Not much, really. He's Hispanic, and he reads. He's also really nice to look at. He's definitely got the tall, dark, and handsome thing down pat. Physically, he's very fit. Those are lean muscles underneath his tight T-shirt. But what I like best about him is that he seems like a genuinely nice, compassionate person.

It's been a long time since I've been around someone, besides Edward, who didn't make me feel defensive or, even worse, like I was a nutjob.

* * *

At five-thirty, I stop work for the day and head for the kitchen. The banana didn't last me long, and I'm so hungry I could eat a horse. Miguel is standing outside on my balcony, checking out the view.

"I think I'll make a pizza for dinner," I say. "Do you want some?" It would be rude of me not to offer.

He steps back inside the apartment. "Yeah, that'd be great. Can I help?"

My pulse kicks up a notch. "Thanks, but no. I've got it." I turn on the kitchen faucet to wash my hands.

Pizza is one of my comfort foods, but it's too expensive to order in, so I've gotten pretty good at making my own. "Is Margherita okay?"

"Sure," he says. "I never met a pizza I didn't like."

I turn on the oven to preheat before I get out a big glass mixing bowl, some flour, yeast, and warm water to make the dough. I'm finding it impossible not to feel self-conscious when Miguel joins me in the kitchen. He leans against the counter with his muscular arms crossed over his chest as he watches me work.

After mixing the dough, I cover the bowl and set it on top of the warm oven. I set a timer. "Now we wait for the dough to rise."

"I'm impressed," he says. "You make your own dough from scratch."

"Necessity is the mother of invention, right? I'm sure you've seen the prices of pizzas in Chicago these days. I can't afford to order in, so I make my own. But before you get too impressed, I will confess that I use pizza sauce from a jar."

"That's the best kind." The corners of his dark eyes crinkle as he grins at me. "Don't worry. Your secret's safe with me."

As he watches me oil the pizza pan, I try not to let it bother me that he's standing so close. It's a bit unnerving.

"You must like plants," he observes as he nods toward the balcony.

I smile. "I do. They make a nice privacy screen. And I like to think I inherited a green thumb."

"Do you ever sit outside on your balcony?" he asks.

"No, never. I only go out there long enough to water my plants."

"Do you miss being outside? Miss the fresh air and sunshine?"

I shake my head. "Sure, but it's not safe."

He looks pensive. "Ruby, do you mind if I ask you some questions?"

I swallow hard. I've been dreading this. "I figured you would."

He smiles apologetically. "I don't mean to pry, but I need to know some things, to better understand the situation. Edward told me you haven't left your apartment in a long time. Is that right?"

I nod. "Not in the two years I've been living here."

"How do you manage everything without ever leaving your apartment?"

"It's not hard. Everything can be delivered these days—groceries, pet food, art supplies, and packaging and mailing supplies."

"How do you mail your paintings?"

"My neighbor, Darren, collects my outgoing packages and takes them downstairs to the mailroom. He also brings me my mail every evening when he returns home from work."

"Darren? Which apartment is his?"

"He lives next door in 2A." I point in the direction of my neighbor's unit. "Darren's been a huge help—besides bringing me my mail, he takes my trash bags to the trash chute at the end of the hall."

"How did you meet this neighbor?"

I pause for a moment, having to think back. "He moved into the building about a year ago. He came by to say hello, and we got to talking."

Miguel looks skeptical. "But how did that lead to him getting your mail for you and taking out your trash?"

"I guess he saw Edward doing it, and he offered to help out. It just sort of grew out of that. Darren didn't seem to mind, and I hated inconveniencing Edward by asking him to come over so often."

"Has Darren ever been inside your apartment?"

"No."

"Has he ever asked to come in?"

I nod. "A few times."

"And you said no?"

"Yeah. I always made up an excuse. Eventually, he quit asking."

"How about groceries? How do you get food?"

"My groceries are delivered each week from a small family-owned grocery store two blocks away—Franklin's Market. Everything else I can order online and have it shipped here. Amazon carries pretty much everything."

"What about doctor's visits?"

"I've never been sick, but if I were, I can do a virtual visit with a doctor online."

He nods. "It sounds like you've got it all figured out."

When the timer goes off, I place the dough on the prepared baking sheet, oil my hands, and start forming the pie. He watches me quietly.

So far he's asking easy questions, but I know the hard ones are coming.

Suddenly, Miguel steps away from the counter, crosses to the pantry, and returns with a jar of pizza sauce, which he sets on the counter.

"Thank you," I say, caught off guard and a bit surprised at his thoughtfulness.

"No problem," he says as he returns to his spot.

After shaping the dough, I wash my hands before popping the pizza pan into the oven to prebake. I set a timer for a few minutes.

"What about you?" I ask. I figure turnabout is fair play. Now it's my turn to ask questions.

"What about me?" he asks, grinning.

I start with an easy one. "How old are you?"

"Thirty."

"Do you like working in security?"

"I love it. It's a fantastic career."

I pick up the jar of pizza sauce and try to open it, but the lid won't budge.

Miguel holds out his hand. As I study his palm and long fingers, I feel a shiver ripple down my spine. I shake myself mentally as I hand him the jar. He pops the lid off effortlessly and hands it back to me.

"Thanks," I say.

"No problem. I really don't mean to pry, but..."

Here they come—the difficult questions.

"Would you mind telling me *why?*"

"Why what?" I ask. "You mean, why don't I leave my apartment? Or why have I shut myself off from the rest of the world?"

Miguel nods, then stands there leaning against the counter, patiently waiting.

5

Ruby

I open a bottle of chilled sparkling water and take a long sip in an effort to buy myself some time. Now we're getting to the stuff I don't want to talk about. The stuff that brings back horrific memories that still haunt me.

When I glance up at him, I'm struck by the depth of compassion I see in his dark eyes. He knows it hurts me to talk about this, and he feels bad for asking.

The oven timer goes off, so I pull the pizza crust out

of the oven and start spreading the sauce. "The world is a cruel and dangerous place."

"It certainly can be," he says. He sighs heavily. "Ruby, I'm really sorry about your mother. Edward told me how she died."

My throat tightens, and I swallow against a painful lump. For a moment, I don't speak. I can't. I don't want to think about what happened to her, let alone talk about it. Tears prick my eyes, and I blink against the pain.

"I can't imagine how horrible it must have been for you," he says. "You were so young."

"I was eight."

"Your godfather told me you witnessed her death."

Feeling sick, I nod. "He shot her right in front of me. I was sitting in the back seat of the car, already buckled into my seat. She was in the process of getting in the driver's seat when he grabbed her and pulled her out. When she started to fight back, he shot her." I shudder at the memory. "He didn't even hesitate."

When I don't say anything more, he fills in the rest for me. "The assailant took off in the car with you in the backseat?"

"Yes. After driving around for hours, he finally let me out at a shopping center. I think he panicked. I don't think he intended to kidnap me. He kept muttering to himself, over and over, about what he was going to do now. Nothing he said made any sense. He was probably on something."

Miguel's eyes soften. "I'm glad you weren't hurt."

"I wasn't hurt physically, no. But emotionally he took everything from me." I meet his penetrating gaze for a split second before looking away. I head to the fridge to retrieve fresh basil leaves and mozzarella.

While I'm putting on the last of the toppings, he asks, "Who else do you interact with, besides your father, Edward, and your neighbor Darren? Anyone else?"

"No, not really."

"I'll need to pay him a visit."

"Who?" I ask.

"Darren."

That's a surprise. "Why?"

"He lives next door to you, and he interacts with you more than anyone else does. That automatically makes him a suspect in my book. At the very least, I have to rule him out."

I shake my head. "It's not Darren."

"Why do you say that?"

"Darren wouldn't hurt a fly. He's—I promise you, it's

not him."

"In this business, I've learned that sometimes the ones you least suspect are the ones who pose the most danger."

I slide the pizza back into the oven and set the timer. "It's definitely not Darren." I laugh. "He's an accountant, not a stalker."

"Tell me what this person does—the one terrorizing you."

"He throws rocks at my window at night when I'm in bed—tiny rocks, more like pebbles, nothing big enough to break the glass. Just big enough to make noise and keep me up at night."

"Anything else?"

"He leaves things on my welcome mat in the night. I find them in the morning."

"Things? Such as?"

"It varies." I shrug. "Sometimes it's a bouquet of dead flowers. Sometimes it's notes. But sometimes it's a dead animal. Roadkill mostly, I think. Squirrels and birds that are half-decomposed." I shudder. "Those are the worst. The smell, and the blood."

"What kind of notes?"

"What do you mean?"

"Are they handwritten or printed?"

"Printed, off a computer, in a large bold font."

"What do they say?"

"They say things like *'we should be together,' 'I love you,'* and *'you're mine.'* Stuff like that."

"Do you still have any of the notes?"

"No. As soon as I get one, I tear it up and throw it away."

"What do you do with the dead animals?"

"I put them in trash bags and leave them outside my door. Darren takes the bags to the trash chute for me."

Miguel frowns. "Darren again."

"It's not Darren." I sigh, not understanding why Miguel is so fixated on my neighbor. "He's a nice guy. He's the closest thing I have to a friend."

"What about the apartment manager? Do you ever interact with him?"

"Not if I can help it. His name is Rick, but I hardly ever see him. My rent gets paid automatically each month, so unless something in the apartment needs fixing, I never have any reason to talk to him. And believe me, that's a good thing. He's awful."

Miguel frowns. "What do you mean, he's awful? Has Rick ever done or said anything inappropriate to you?"

"He's just an awful person. He's been in my apartment a few times since I moved in to fix things, and he always insinuates that the problems are my fault. He resents having to fix anything—clogged drains, loose outlets, leaky windows. He's nosey, and he's in everyone's business. He says no to everything. Some of the tenants wanted to decorate their doors, and he said no. No one likes him."

"Do you talk to any other neighbors besides Darren?"

"No."

I finally muster the courage to meet Miguel's gaze. "Do you think this is all in my head?"

"I don't have an opinion yet. I need evidence before I can make any kind of determination."

"My father thinks it's all in my head. He thinks I'm crazy. Or that I'm making this up for attention. Trust me, the last thing I want is attention."

"From what I hear, your father's not the most open-minded person."

I chuckle. "That's an understatement."

"What about Edward? He seems like a great guy."

"He is. He's the only one who gives me unconditional support. My mom met both my dad and Edward when she was in college. In fact, she dated both of them. In the end, she married my dad, but still, she and Edward remained close friends, even after they all graduated. I don't think Edward and my father liked each other very much, then or now."

"Why do you say that?"

"My parents fought a lot, and sometimes it was about Edward. I would hide in my bedroom closet during their many screaming matches, but I could still hear bits and pieces of what they were arguing about. Edward's name came up a lot."

"Your mom and Edward… was there ever anything going on between them? They sound like they were pretty close."

"I don't think so. Edward and my mother truly loved each other, but it was definitely a platonic sort of love. I think she got more emotional support from him than from my father, and my dad resented it."

When the kitchen timer goes off, Miguel grabs the oven mitt. "I'll get it."

I step back as he opens the oven and pulls out the pizza pan. He sets it on top of the stove.

While the pizza cools a bit, Miguel offers to help me set the table. It's weird because I'm not used to having help. I hand him plates and silverware, and he puts them on the table.

Miguel opens the fridge. "What would you like to drink?"

"I have sparkling water. I've got beer in there if you want one. Help yourself."

"Thanks, but no. I'm on duty. No alcohol. Sparkling water is fine."

I guess that means he won't be drinking any alcohol for the foreseeable future—at least as long as he's here. He may regret that.

After I cut the pizza, Miguel brings over our plates, and I lay two slices on each one. He carries our plates back to the table, and I grab our drinks. I'm struck by how well we work together, how naturally it comes. It's kind of nice having help.

Miguel takes a bite of his pizza and moans dramatically, making me laugh. "This is really good. You could definitely give the pizzerias in town a run for their money."

"Thanks. It's no Gino's or Giordano's, but it hits the spot."

Miguel initiates conversation at the table, asking me about the neighborhood, asking me how I like Wicker Park. He tells me he has friends in the neighborhood—a woman, Molly, who owns an art studio. "You should meet her sometime. I think you'd like her. The book I was reading earlier was written by her fiancé, Jamie McIntyre. He's a former Navy SEAL, now an author of military thrillers."

After we're done devouring the pizza, we clear the table and carry our dishes to the sink.

"Do you prefer to wash or dry?" he asks.

"You're offering to help?"

"Of course. In my family, everyone pitches in. I've been washing dishes since I was tall enough to reach the sink."

"Thanks. I'll wash, if you don't mind." I pull a clean kitchen towel out of a drawer and hand it to him. Then I fill the sink with hot soapy water and start washing. "Do you have a big family?" I don't know why I'm asking him personal questions, but it's so easy to talk to him.

"I'm the oldest of eight kids—four boys and four girls. Then there's my parents, all four grandparents, and more aunts, uncles, and cousins than I can count. Most of us live here in Chicago. We're a pretty tight knit group."

"I can't imagine having that much family around. I'm an only child, so it's just me and my—my dad. And mostly now it's just me." I frown. "For my birthday last year, Edward brought me a cake he made himself. My father forgot entirely."

Miguel's smile falls. "That's awful."

Mentally, I shake myself. "No, it's fine."

"Are you done working for the day?" he asks as he dries one of our plates and places it in the cupboard.

"Yes. The painting needs to dry thoroughly before I can seal it."

"So, how do you spend your evenings?" he asks. "What do you do for fun?"

"I either read or watch something on TV. How about you?"

"Same," he says. "In my line of work, I don't get a lot of free time, so when I do, I'm usually chilling in my apartment, reading, watching something, or working out. My buddies and I have a standing thing we do Friday evenings after work. We meet up at Tanks—it's a local pub."

I imagine Miguel has a lot of friends. He's friendly and easy to talk to. It dawns on me that today's Friday. "Tonight's Friday. Are you going to meet your friends?"

"No, not tonight. I'm sticking right here with you."

"I'm sorry you're going to miss seeing your friends this evening."

"It's okay." He dries the other plate and puts it in the cupboard. "You're more important."

When I glance up at him, I find him gazing down at me. "I am?"

He nods. "Yes, you are."

I don't know if it's his words or the way he's looking at me, but my pulse starts racing again. This time in a good way.

6

Miguel

After we finish with the dishes, Ruby disappears into her bedroom to change. While she's doing that, I take a minute to catch up on text messages and e-mails from work. One of the texts I received is from Shane, who's checking in and wanting to know what I've discovered so far.

> **Me – Nothing yet. She needs a security system in her apartment. I'm going to talk to the building mgr about putting cameras in the hallway outside her apt. so I can see who's coming and going.**

Shane – I'll ask Jake to get one installed ASAP.

I have nothing to go on yet. Ruby's given me a lot of vague examples, but she has no proof to back up any of her claims. It's understandable that she'd dispose of any evidence as soon as she got it—the notes, the roadkill. Now it's my job to collect evidence—if any exists. I'm keeping an open mind. Ruby doesn't seem the fanciful type, so even though there's no evidence to back up any of her claims, I'm inclined to believe her. I'll at least give her the benefit of the doubt.

I make a mental list of the people I need to speak to—for starters, her helpful neighbor Darren and the apartment manager, Rick. I also need to interview the other residents who live on this floor. Any one of them might have seen something suspicious, or *someone*, and not realized it.

Do I think this stalker is all in Ruby's head? It's too soon to tell.

I don't blame her for being so fearful of the world. She witnessed something horrific, and it had a lasting impact on her. It's not surprising that she'd internalize the idea that the world is a dangerous place. Her world—her sense of security—was shattered when she was young and impressionable.

After I catch up on work stuff, I realize my muscles are stiff from inactivity. I wish I had my home gym equipment here so I could get in a good workout. Barring that, I'd love to go for a run, but I can't leave Ruby alone. Not yet. Not until I have a better understanding of what we're dealing with. So I do the next best thing—I hop up from the sofa to do some old-school calisthenics. I drop down onto the floor and power through a hundred pushups, followed by just as many sit-ups. And that's just for starters.

Man, I'd give anything for a set of free weights or a treadmill right now. If this assignment looks like it's going to continue for a while, I might have to bring some hand weights over. I doubt there's room for a treadmill.

While I put my body through the motions, my brain works through what little I know about Ruby's case. It's entirely possible that this stalker is a figment of her imagination. I'm prepared for that. I'm also prepared for the possibility that there is someone out there who's terrorizing this poor girl. If there is—he'd better watch out. I don't tolerate bullies.

After finishing my impromptu exercise regimen, I get out my laptop and surf the Internet.

My phone chimes with an incoming message from

Shane's brother Jake, who's in charge of surveillance for the company.

Jake – I'm sending Philip over w/a security system ETA 30 mins

Ruby comes out of the bathroom with her face freshly washed and flushed a light pink. Her hair is up in a ponytail, making her look even younger. Her eyes are bright, and I love her freckles.

Damn. She's pretty.

She eyes me curiously. "Is something wrong?"

I look back at my laptop screen so I'm not staring at her. The last thing I need is for her to feel self-conscious around me. "I was just thinking we should install a security system in your apartment. I also want surveillance cameras installed in the hallway so I have visibility on your door."

She frowns. "You'll have to talk to Rick about the cameras. He's really funny about letting us put things in the hallway. We had to get everyone in the building to sign a petition just so we could put welcome mats in front of our doors."

"I'll talk to him tomorrow about the cameras. In the meantime, we need to install a security system in your apartment." I give her a minute to let that sink in. "Is that okay with you?"

She seems wary. "I suppose so."

"Great. I'll have someone come over this evening to install it."

Ruby's eyes widen and the blood practically drains from her face. "Come here? Tonight?"

"Hey, it's okay." I rise from the table and take a step toward her. My impulse is to reassure her—comfort her—but I stop myself. I doubt she'd want a hug from me right now. "His name is Philip Underwood, and he's a personal friend of mine. There's absolutely nothing to worry about, I promise."

Suddenly, there's a light rap on Ruby's door.

"That's Darren stopping by with my mail." Ruby walks up to the door and looks through the peephole. "It's Darren." She unlocks the door but leaves the chain.

I walk up behind her to get a look at her neighbor.

"Hi, Darren," she says, seeming perfectly at ease with the guy.

"Hi, Ruby," says the blond man standing outside her door. He's dressed in a tan suit and white dress shirt, no tie. He slips a small stack of envelopes through the opening.

"Thanks," she says.

Darren finally directs his attention at me. He stares at me a moment, his brow furrowing, before he turns his gaze back to Ruby. "Is everything okay, Ruby?"

She nods. "Yes, fine."

Darren scowls my way. "Who is this guy?"

Ruby glances back at me and smiles. "Oh," she replies, clearly caught off guard. "This is my friend, Miguel."

Darren's scowl morphs into a glare. "Friend? Since when? How did you meet this guy?"

Ruby looks helplessly back at me. "Well—I—he's a friend of my godfather. You've met Edward before. He's a friend of Edward's."

There's skepticism written all over Darren's face. "Really."

"That's right," she says, starting to recover. "I met him through Edward."

"What's he doing here?"

"He's visiting," Ruby says.

Darren looks more than a bit agitated now. "For how long?"

Ruby shrugs. "I'm not sure. As long as he wants, I guess." She chuckles, but there's a detectable quaver in the sound. "Thanks for bringing up my mail, Darren. I appreciate it." And then she gives him a dismissive nod, softened by a smile, and starts to close the door.

Darren blocks the door with his foot. "Ruby, wait."

"What is it?"

He leans close and whispers. "Are you sure you're okay?"

"I'm fine. Thanks for bringing my mail." She pushes the door closed, locks the deadbolts, and turns to lean against the door. "Oh, my God. That was awkward."

I watch as she rifles through her mail. "Junk mail, junk mail, junk mail, credit card application. It's all junk." She walks to the kitchen and tosses the mail into a box marked SHRED.

"From now on, I'll collect your mail, okay?"

"Sure. If you don't mind."

"Not at all." I head for the door and start to unlock the deadbolts. "I'll be right back. Why don't you lock up after I leave?"

"Wait! Where are you going?" Ruby asks as she joins me at the door. Her voice is laced with panic.

"I'm going to have a talk with your neighbor."

"Who? Darren?"

"Yes. I want to feel him out. Besides, I'll let him know I'll be getting your mail from now on."

"No!" She grabs my wrist. "Don't go out there, please."

I lower my arm and face her. "Why not?"

She looks truly afraid. Her voice drops to a whisper. "You know why. It's not safe."

My chest tightens, and I realize it's because I hurt for Ruby. I stare down at her pale expression, her eyes filled with panic. She's practically paralyzed with fear. It's sad because she's missing out on so much in life. She's young and talented and beautiful. She should be out in the world living her best life and experiencing all the good the world has to offer, not trapped here inside her apartment, living a life devoid of sunshine and fresh air.

I pry her grip from my wrist and squeeze her hand. "I'll be fine, Ruby. There's nothing to worry about. I'm just going next door to pay Darren a friendly visit. That's all. What's his last name?"

"Ingles." Ruby still doesn't look happy. In fact, she looks like she's about to jump out of her skin.

"You can lock the door after I leave," I tell her, but I have a feeling that's a given.

She nods.

And then I let myself out of the apartment. Before I take a step toward Darren's unit, I hear all three deadbolts locking, one right after another. Then I hear the chain slide into place.

Darren's apartment, 2A, is to the left of Ruby's unit. I walk to his door and knock. The door opens almost immediately.

His suit jacket is off, and his shirt collar is unbuttoned. "Yes?" He's glaring at me. "What do you want?"

There's a lot of unjustified hostility in his voice. The guy doesn't even know me. He has no reason to dislike me.

Unless he's jealous that I'm in Ruby's apartment. He's never made it past her threshold.

"Darren, we need to talk."

7

Miguel

Darren's eyes narrow on me. "Talk about what?"

"Ruby. Who do you think?"

"What's your business with Ruby?" he asks.

"She told you—I'm a friend. I'm just visiting."

"That's bullshit. Ruby doesn't have any friends."

Since I can't really refute that, I ignore it. "Ruby tells me you've been helping her out with mail and trash."

"Yes. So?"

"I wanted to thank you. I'm sure you know Ruby

doesn't get out much."

Darren frowns as he tries to figure out where this is going. "It's no big deal," he says. "Ruby's a sweet girl. I'm happy to help her out."

I nod. "I appreciate it. I was wondering, have you noticed anyone hanging around Ruby's apartment door? Maybe leaving things on her welcome mat?"

"No."

"I see. Well, if you notice anything odd, would you let me know? And, now that I'm here, I'll take care of Ruby's mail and trash." I pull a fake business card from my back pocket and hand it to him. It contains just my name and cell number, no other identifying information. "Here's my number. If you see anything suspicious, give me a call."

As I walk away, he calls after me, "Hey, I don't mind helping her out. It's no problem. I'm happy to do it."

"That won't be necessary. I'll take care of anything she needs."

Scowling, Darren closes his door and locks it.

Well, that wasn't weird at all. Unfortunately, I can't strike Darren off my list of suspects. The guy seems a bit possessive where Ruby's concerned.

Before returning to the apartment, I make a quick

detour and head downstairs to the front lobby, where the mail room is located. I easily find Ruby's mail compartment, 2B, built into the wall. The mail room is pretty bare... just the boxes for the tenants, a white plastic chair, and a trash can filled with junk mail.

It's easy to see how someone could slip an envelope into her mailbox. These old mailboxes aren't secure. They all contain slots so the mail carrier can just slide the mail into each box.

I glance out the front window at the street, which is bustling with traffic. There's a steady flow of pedestrians on the sidewalk, most of them likely on their way home from work. Ruby lives in a mixed-use area, combining apartments with small businesses and restaurants. Across the street from Ruby's building is an old Catholic church with a tall steeple. It's the top of the hour, and the church bell rings seven times. A couple of blocks away is a large playground.

On my way back upstairs to Ruby, I get a text message from my friend Philip.

Philip – On my way. I'll be there in ten.

Me – thanks

I race up the stairs and knock quietly on Ruby's door. "Ruby, it's me, Miguel. I'm back."

A moment later, she unlocks the door and opens it. I slip inside, and immediately she relocks the door.

"How was your meeting with Darren?" she asks.

"Inconclusive. He's an interesting guy. How much do you know about him?"

She shrugs. "Not much. He's an accountant."

"That's it? That's all you know?"

"Pretty much. We don't really talk much. He just brings me my mail and takes away my trash."

"Okay. By the way, my friend will be here soon to install the security system." She doesn't look happy, so I add, "It's for your protection, Ruby. If anyone were to try to break in, the police would be notified immediately. There's also a panic button that you can use to instantly summon emergency services—police, fire, or paramedics. I'll be here with you the entire time he's installing the system. It'll be quick and painless, I promise."

Those crystal-clear blue eyes glance up at me, and indecision is written all over her face. Impulsively, I reach for her hand, but she steps back.

"It's in your best interest, Ruby. If I had to leave for any reason, you'd be perfectly safe here. The door and all the windows would be armed with sensors."

She nods reluctantly. "Okay."

"Good. He'll be here any minute."

Her eyes widen, but she doesn't say anything.

A few minutes later, there's a knock at the door.

"That'll be Philip," I tell her. "I'll get it." I open the door and let him in. He's loaded down with a box and a tool kit.

Ruby takes one look at Philip—he's a mountain of a man at six-six—and points down the hall. "I'm sorry, but I have to—" And then she looks at me. "I have work to do." Ruby rushes off and disappears into her studio, closing the door behind her.

I hate putting her on the spot like this. She had little warning that Philip was coming over so soon. Two strangers in her apartment now in one day—that's a lot for her to deal with.

Philip sets his supplies down. "She doesn't seem too happy that I'm here."

I sigh. "Yeah, she's not comfortable around strangers."

"I'll get right on this so I can get out of your hair." Phil gets busy installing the main control panel beside the door. Then he moves quickly through the apartment attaching sensors on each window. He does the kitchen window, the balcony doors, the living room window, and Ruby's bedroom window. He saves the art studio for last. We both stand in front of the closed door.

"You want to tell her I need in here?" he asks.

I knock, then open the door wide enough to poke my head in. "If you don't mind, Philip needs to come in here to install the last window sensor."

Ruby jumps up from her chair and walks out of the studio, disappearing into her bedroom.

After attaching the last window sensor, he configures the main control panel. "What four digits do you want me to use for her access code?"

"Good question. Just a sec." I head down the hallway and knock on her bedroom door. "Ruby? Can I come in?"

The door opens, and she's right there, peering up at me. "Yes? Is he gone?"

"Not quite. I need to know your birthday."

"August 30th."

"Thanks." And then I head back to Phil, who's waiting by the control panel. "Make it zero-eight-three-zero." That'll be easy for her to remember. She can always change it later if she wants to.

After Phil tests each of the sensors, he leaves. I set up the monitoring app on my phone for the security system. I'll need to set the app up on Ruby's phone, too.

I wait for Ruby to come out of her room, but she

doesn't seem to be in any hurry. I knock on her door. "Ruby?"

There's no answer.

I try again, knocking quietly. "Ruby, he's gone. You can come out now."

Still nothing.

She's overwhelmed—too many strangers in her space lately. First me, and then Philip.

So I sit on the floor and lean on her door. "I'll wait until you feel like coming out."

When I hear the quiet shuffle of footsteps, I suspect she's close to the door. Maybe even sitting on the other side. "I know it was stressful having a stranger—another stranger—in your apartment, but it's worth it. You'll be so much safer now. No one can get into your apartment without your knowledge. And if he does, the police will be summoned."

"You believe me?" Her voice is muffled through the door, so quiet I almost didn't hear her.

"Yeah, I do." The truth is I don't know anything with certainty—not yet anyway. There's no indisputable evidence of a stalker, but I'm not going to tell her that. Right now she needs to feel like someone believes her. More than anything, she needs a friend.

I feel bad for stressing her out. "How about we watch a movie?"

A full minute passes with no response. Then her bedroom doorknob turns, and the door opens. I jump to my feet and face her.

She tucks a strand of hair behind her ear and nods. "Sure. I'll watch a movie with you."

I motion for her to proceed down the hallway to the living room. "What do you want to watch?"

When she glances back at me, her waterfall of red hair bounces over her shoulder. I see only her profile, a soft round cheek with scattered freckles, a partial curving lip. "What kind of movies do you like?"

I shrug. "Action and sci-fi, mostly. Or thrillers." I wonder what she's into. Romantic comedies? Jane Austen? Most of the ladies love those Jane Austen movies.

Her nose wrinkles as she considers my question. "I have a suggestion. How about an action film about a giant shark?"

I can't help laughing because it's so unexpected. "You mean *Jaws*?"

"Sort of, but from this century. It stars Jason Statham. He's a big action hero."

"I know who he is. Sure, that sounds good."

We sit on the sofa, and Ruby reaches for the remote. She calls up a streaming service and locates a movie called *The Meg*. We watch the trailer, and it looks like it's got a little bit of everything—action, suspense, a giant shark, and yes, a little bit of romance. I figured there'd be some romance in there somewhere.

As the movie starts, she asks, "Would you like a beer?"

I shake my head. "Still on duty."

"But it's late. Surely your workday is over."

"It's never over."

She gets up, walks to the kitchen, and pulls a bottle of sparkling water out of the fridge. "Would you like one of these?"

"Sure. Thanks."

She returns to the sofa, hands me my water, and sits, leaving plenty of space between us. She puts her feet up on the coffee table and wiggles her toes in her socks. "Take your boots off and make yourself comfortable."

"That's okay."

"Because you're on duty?"

"Yeah. I might have to move fast, you know? If something happens."

The movie starts, and we turn our attention to the screen. But Ruby seems a bit tense. She flinches at every single noise she hears—neighbors' doors opening and closing, the sound of a young child crying next door, a dog barking, footsteps in the hallway. She's hypervigilant, but I guess that's to be expected under the circumstances.

I watch her profile out of my peripheral vision, noting that she's sitting as far away from me as possible. Her arms are crossed over her chest. I hate that she lives in this constant state of anxiety. I need some clear evidence soon so I can confirm her claims and ID the perpetrator.

It's the least I can do for her.

A door slams somewhere on this floor of the building, and Ruby jumps. Immediately, she looks at me, but doesn't say anything. It's almost as if she's saying, "You heard that, too, right?"

I don't think she trusts her own judgment anymore.

8

Ruby

I love this movie, and I've seen it before. That's a good thing because right now I'm doing a lousy job of paying attention. Even though we're sitting at opposite ends of the sofa, I can't help being distracted by Miguel's presence.

There's a man in my apartment. And, he's not leaving anytime soon. In fact, he'll be spending the night—maybe many nights.

I watch him out of the corner of my eye. He's got the

ankle of one foot casually propped up on his other knee. One arm is resting on the sofa arm. Even though we're sitting several feet apart, I can *feel* his presence.

When a door slams down the hall from my apartment, I jump. I look at Miguel to see if he noticed, but his attention is on the TV screen.

He downs his sparkling water pretty quickly and sets the empty bottle on a coaster on the coffee table.

"Would you like another one?" I ask.

"Thanks, but no. I'm good."

Pumpkin jumps up on the sofa to join us. He walks across my lap, then goes to check out Miguel. He ends up curling up on the sofa between us. I smile when I notice Miguel reaching over to rub Pumpkin's belly.

The movie's intense at times, keeping me on my toes. But I jump for real every time I hear a noise coming from outside my apartment. I hear people walking down the hall, voices, a dog barking in another apartment. These noises are typical, but for some reason, having Miguel here makes them seem a bit less threatening.

When the movie ends and the credits roll, Miguel says, "That was good."

I cover my mouth when I yawn. "I'm glad you liked it." I stand and collect our empty bottles. "It's getting late. I guess I'll head to bed."

He stands and stretches, arching his back and extending his muscular arms with a deep groan. "Is there anything I can help with?"

I gesture toward the kitchen. "You could put these in the recycling bin, while I grab some bedding for the sofa."

Miguel disposes of the empty bottles, then joins me at the linen closet, where I grab a pillow, sheets, and a blanket.

He takes them from me. "I'll make up the bed."

As I stand this close to him, he seems even taller than I remember. "If you need anything, just let me know."

"I'll be fine," he says, giving me a gentle smile. "If you hear anything in the night, come get me, okay? That's why I'm here."

"Okay." If something does happen, I'm glad I don't have to deal with it alone. "If you get hungry—" I point toward the kitchen "—help yourself."

He nods patiently. "Don't worry, I will. Sleep well."

"All right, then. Good night." I nod toward my bedroom. "I guess I'll hit the hay."

To my surprise, I'm finding it hard to tear myself away from him. I'm not used to having company. Or companionship. Or even a friend. It feels... good.

As I walk away, he remains standing in the same spot, watching me go, as if it's his job to be sure I make it to my bedroom okay.

After I make a pit stop in the bathroom to pee and brush my teeth, I head to my bedroom and change into my nightgown. Pumpkin's already curled up at the foot of my bed. He lifts his head, one eye opening partway, then lies back down. As soon as I slide between the cool sheets, he gets up and resettles next to me, pressing against my side.

"G'night, Punkie." When I scratch the back of his neck, he starts purring.

My bedroom is nearly pitch black at night thanks to the light-blocking drapes hanging in the window. They're thick, heavy drapes designed to block out not just light but also sound. Sometimes the parking lot behind the building can get a bit noisy late at night, even into the wee hours, especially on weekends.

I reach over to open the top drawer of my nightstand and open my bottle of melatonin. I pop a cherry-flavored tablet into my mouth and let it dissolve under my tongue.

The apartment is quiet, and I wonder if Miguel is in

bed yet. Is he one of those people who goes to bed early and gets up early, or is he a night owl?

The apartment is so quiet.

Is he reading?

On his phone?

Texting his friends about this weird new assignment of his?

Is he bored?

Does he regret agreeing to this job?

My mind races with lots of questions and concerns and zero answers.

I hope he can get comfortable on the sofa. I know it's fine to sleep on because I've slept on it many times. I'm just worried because there's no way he can stretch out fully—it's not long enough for him.

I should have offered to let him use my bed, because I fit just fine on the sofa. I've slept on it on those nights when *he* keeps throwing pebbles at my window, and I can't sleep.

I stroke Pumpkin's back. "There's a stranger sleeping on our sofa."

Pumpkin stretches and lets out a chirping sound. I think he approves of our house guest.

"He seems nice," I say. "You seemed to like him well

enough."

I thought I'd have a harder time having someone in my apartment, but Miguel's so nice, he's easy to have around. There's something about him. He seems to exude an air of quiet confidence, and that's really an attractive trait in a man.

I start in on my breathing exercises in an effort to calm my pulse and relax so I can sleep.

I repeat my mantra to myself, over and over.

It's okay.

Everything's okay.

You're safe.

And it works. I feel my pulse gradually slowing and my muscles relaxing. My eyelids start to grow heavy.

* * *

When I wake up, I check the time. It's just after seven-thirty. It's the first time I slept through the night in a long time. I didn't hear a sound. Not the *ping* of a pebble hitting my window. No thump of something heavy hitting my apartment door. Nothing.

I can't remember the last time I had a quiet, uneventful night.

I wonder what Miguel thinks. I'm so afraid he'll think it's all in my head.

I sit up and turn on the bedside lamp. Pumpkin squints at me and rolls onto his back, stretching his torso.

"I actually slept through the night," I say. Pumpkin jumps off the bed and walks to the door. "I know, I know. You want breakfast. Just a minute."

I listen carefully for any signs that Miguel is up, but I don't hear anything. I need to visit the bathroom, but I'd hate to wake him up if he's still asleep. That's the downside to sleeping on the sofa—you have no privacy at all.

But my bladder is insistent, so I get out of bed, throw on my robe, and quietly let myself out of my room. As soon as I step out of my bedroom, I see there's a light on in the living room. I walk in that direction and find Miguel dressed and sitting on the chair by the sofa. He's back to reading his book.

"Good morning," I say.

He glances. "Good morning. I hope you slept well."

"Actually, I did. It was a quiet night."

After I get washed up and dressed, I return to the living room to find Miguel in the kitchen making coffee.

I feed Pumpkin, who's meowing eagerly as he winds himself around my ankles. "I'm making scrambled eggs and toast for breakfast. Would you like some?"

"Yes, please," he says.

While I make breakfast, I can't help wondering what he's thinking about. Last night was a perfectly normal, perfectly quiet night. Nothing went bump in the night. I wonder if he's starting to doubt my claims.

As I carry our food to the table, Miguel opens the balcony drapes. "Do you mind if I open the door?"

"Go right ahead."

As soon as he slides the door open, I feel a slight breeze and hear the birds chirping in the trees across the parking lot.

Miguel brings the coffee pot to the table and pours us each a cup. "How do you like your coffee?"

"Sugar and cream. Sugar's on the table. Creamer's in the fridge. I'll get it."

Miguel sits and takes a bite of his scrambled eggs. "These are good."

I nod as I pour some French vanilla creamer into my coffee and offer him the bottle, but he declines.

"I drink it black, thanks." He watches me for a moment. "You're awfully quiet this morning. Is everything okay?"

I nod as I take a sip of my coffee. I can still feel his gaze on me. "Nothing happened last night."

He nods as he takes another bite of food. After he swallows, he says, "Is that a good thing or bad?"

"I'm just wondering what you're thinking."

"About what?"

"The stalker. I'm afraid you'll think I made it up."

He sets his coffee mug down. "No, I don't think you made it up. I really don't have an opinion yet."

I realize I have nothing to show for my claims, not one shred of evidence. In hindsight, I wish I'd kept the notes, but at the time they creeped me out, and I just wanted to get rid of them. As for the dead animals, I should have shown the roadkill to Darren before I had him throw them away. Then I'd have a witness. I've been so stupid. I missed so many opportunities to gather evidence. And now when I have someone here, someone willing to believe me, I have nothing to show him.

"Ruby?"

Startled, I glance at Miguel. "I'm sorry, what?"

"I asked you what's wrong?"

"I just realized that I should have kept the notes and taken pictures of the roadkill. Then I'd have proof. Or, I could have shown it to Darren. Then I'd have a witness. But instead, I have nothing."

"Hey, it's okay. People generally don't think about things like that when they're scared. Don't worry. We'll get the evidence."

I wish I was as optimistic as he is.

After breakfast, Miguel demonstrates how to arm and disarm the new security system. The security code is my birthday, which makes it easy.

"The alarm is tied in to a twenty-four-seven call center at McIntyre Security. If it goes off, they'll call you to ask if everything's okay. Honestly, most alarm events are simply accidents. Just give them your code word—pumpkin—and they'll cancel the alarm. If you don't answer their call, or if you don't give them the correct code word, they'll summon the police immediately. If you're under duress—if there's someone in here with you—give the call center an incorrect code word. That will tip them off that you need help."

He makes me practice arming and disarming the system a few times. Then he installs an app on my phone and shows me how to use it to control the system remotely—like from my bedroom.

"Will you be all right on your own for a little while?" he asks. "I'd like to go talk to your building manager about putting cameras in the hallway."

"Sure, I'll be fine. I need to get to work anyway."

"Where can I find him?"

"Either in the office or in the maintenance room. Both are on the ground floor."

I nod. "I won't be gone long," he says, and then he lets himself out the door.

I lock up after him and head to my studio.

9

Miguel

The apartment manager's office, which is located across the lobby from the mailroom, is locked. There's a "BE BACK SOON" sign hanging on the door. So I go in search of the maintenance room, which is just around the corner on the ground floor. That door is wide open, and I hear a loud banging sound coming from inside the room.

I knock on the door frame and walk inside to find a man dressed in a pair of dirty overalls standing at a workbench, hammering a piece of metal. He's lanky, with thinning brown hair and brown eyes. "Are you Rick?"

The man stops hammering and glances up. "Yeah." He looks me over and narrows his eyes. "Who's asking?"

Wow, great social skills with this one. "The name's Miguel Rodriguez. I'm a friend of Ruby Foster up in apartment 2B. She's been having some issues lately, and I was hoping I could put some surveillance cameras in the hallway outside her door."

"What kind of issues?"

I'm not divulging anything to this guy. "It's personal."

Rick frowns. "Cameras? Hell no."

"They're really small. No one will even notice them."

He shakes his head adamantly. "It's a violation of people's privacy."

"Look, someone's harassing Ruby. I just want to see who comes to her door, that's all. I'm not spying on her neighbors."

Rick takes a step toward me. "I said no. This is private property, so what I say goes. End of discussion." He resumes his work.

I leave Rick to his hammering and head back toward the stairs just as a young blonde woman attempts to come down. She's standing at the top of the steps clutching a small child in one arm and carrying an umbrella stroller in her other hand. She takes one wavering step as she tries to balance herself.

I rush up to meet her. "Here, let me help you."

Smiling gratefully, she hands me the stroller, freeing up one hand so she can grasp the railing. "Thank you so much."

I carry the stroller down to the lobby, while she follows after me with her little boy in her arms.

"It's a shame we don't have an elevator in this building," she says as she sets the child in the stroller and buckles him in.

"Yeah, a lot of these older buildings don't have them. I'm Miguel, by the way. I'm here visiting Ruby Foster in 2B. Do you know her?"

"I'm Becky." She tucks her hair behind her ear. "I live right next door, in 2C." She shakes her head. "I rarely see anyone coming or going from 2B."

"Have you ever seen anyone loitering outside her apartment or leaving anything outside the door?"

She thinks for a minute. "She has groceries delivered regularly. Those bags are left at her door. And I see the blond guy who lives down the hall picking up trash bags outside her door. I've seen an older guy stop by a few times. But other than that, no. Sorry."

"What about Rick, the building manager? Do you ever see him hanging around her door?"

"Yeah, sometimes. He's a real busybody, you know? He's always trying to stick his nose in everyone's business."

"Can I give you my card?" I pull out my wallet and hand her my card. "If you do see anything or anyone hanging around her door, would you please let me know?"

She tucks my card into her purse. "Sure."

I open the front door for Becky, and she rolls her son out onto the sidewalk. Since I'm down here, I check Ruby's mailbox and find a few envelopes in there. I pull them out and rifle through them. It's mostly junk mail again, which is typical, and her cell phone bill. But there's nothing weird or suspicious.

I jog up the stairs and knock on Ruby's door. "It's me, Miguel."

A moment later, I hear the deadbolts turning, followed by the chain sliding free. She opens the door, and I step inside, closing the door behind me.

She turns all the locks. "Is that my mail?"

"Yes." I hand her the mail and watch as she flips through the envelopes.

She frowns, which makes me think she might be disappointed that there's nothing suspicious. "Did you talk to Rick?"

"I did. He said no to the cameras."

She frowns. "I was afraid of that."

"I met one of your neighbors, a young woman named Becky. I asked her if she's seen anyone hanging around your door. She mentioned Darren and Rick and the guy who delivers your groceries, but no one else. Certainly nothing out of place. She seems nice, though."

"I watch her sometimes playing with her son in the park." Her smile fades, leaving her looking wistful and sad.

"What's wrong?"

"Watching her reminds me of what's missing in my life—a partner, a child. When I was a kid—before I lost my mom—I always assumed I'd have those things one day, but now I can't see it happening."

"You don't know that," I say.

A shadow crosses over her blue eyes. "Who would put up with a recluse like me?"

Plenty of men would, I want to say. I have no doubt men would be beating down her door if they knew she existed. Darren's certainly trying his best to ingratiate himself with her. "Ruby, you're an amazing young woman. I'm sure—"

"I'm a paranoid mental case."

"No, you're not. Who gave you that idea?"

Her cheeks flush. "How about my own father?"

"Well, he's wrong." Impulsively, I reach out and grab her hand. "Don't believe him." I glance down at her hand resting in mine. This time she doesn't pull away. I notice her ring—the square-cut ruby. "Tell me about your ring." I have a feeling it holds special meaning for her. After all, it's a *ruby*. That's no coincidence.

She smiles sadly. "It was my mother's ring. Rubies were her favorite gemstone." She laughs softly. "I guess that's why she named me Ruby. After she died, I asked for the ring." She gazes down at it. "I never saw my mom take this ring off, not once. I don't either. It helps me feel connected to her."

My heart aches for Ruby. I can't imagine the pain she must feel. "Ruby—"

Abruptly, she tugs her hand free. "I'm sorry, but I have to get back to work now." She takes a few steps back. "I'm so far behind schedule."

As she walks away, I say, "I'll see you at lunch, right? You've got to eat."

She nods but doesn't say anything. Pumpkin jumps down from the sofa and hurries after her.

I know how he feels. I don't like watching her walk away either.

I'm tempted to go after her, to make up some lame excuse for needing to talk to her, but I know I shouldn't distract her when she needs to work. So I grab a cold drink from the fridge and get comfortable on the sofa. I can't stop thinking about what she said—about wanting a family of her own and thinking it's impossible. She has no idea how mistaken she is. Any man would feel damn lucky to be in her life.

My chest tightens when I realize I'd put myself in that category.

10

Ruby

I'm a coward for running off the way I did. But it was just too much when he held my hand. My body lit up like a Christmas tree—shivers and tingles radiated up my arm and throughout my body.

Once I'm sitting at my worktable, I clip the reference photo for my new commission—a long-haired calico cat named Marcy—and stare at the blank canvas. I brush a basecoat onto the little four-inch square canvas before I dip my flat brush into an off-white paint that's going to be the background. But instead of putting paint to the canvas, I end up staring out the window at the trees across the parking lot.

The weather started off really nice this morning, but now I see storm clouds rolling in from the west. I hope it rains. I love summer showers, especially when there's lightning—as long as we don't lose electricity. Bad weather makes me appreciate my apartment. At least in here I am safe and dry.

I gaze down at the ring on my right hand. My hand still tingles from when Miguel held it in his. I can't believe I told him about my yearning for a family of my own. I've never told anyone that. I've never even spoken those words aloud. What in the world possessed me to tell *him* of all people?

He has that effect on me. I feel safe telling him things because I know he won't use them against me. It's just not in his nature. I've only known him for forty-eight hours, and yet I feel like I *know* him. That I can trust him.

I think this is what it's like to have a friend.

Pumpkin jumps up onto my work table and swishes his tail around with such enthusiasm he almost knocks my water jar over. "Whoa, buddy!" I steady the jar in time to prevent a disaster.

"All right, concentrate," I tell myself. "Get back to work and quit mooning over—just focus, Ruby!"

But no matter how hard I try, part of my mind is fixated on the guy in the other room. I keep wondering what he's doing—he's probably on his laptop or his phone, or maybe reading. I can't help thinking how lucky any woman would be to have someone like him in her life.

I dip my brush into the off-white paint and start dabbing it on the canvas.

Sometime later, when my stomach starts growling, I leave my studio and head for the kitchen. Miguel's sitting at the dining table, doing something on his laptop.

"Time for lunch," I say. "How about turkey and cheese sandwiches?"

He closes the lid on his laptop and stands. "Sounds good. What can I do?"

"How about setting the table?" I ask.

We eat our sandwiches with chips and fresh strawberries.

"I'm sorry you're stuck here with me," I say. "If you want to go run some errands, you can. I have the security system now, so I'll be fine."

"Actually, I'm enjoying the downtime. It's a nice change of pace. Usually, I'm on the run nonstop with clients."

After lunch, we do the dishes together, and then I disappear back into my studio to work.

The rest of the afternoon passes quickly, and we make burgers for dinner.

That evening, we relax in the living room and read—me on the sofa and Miguel in the armchair. It's nice having someone to sit quietly with.

Suddenly it occurs to me that I don't know very much about him. "How long have you worked for McIntyre Security?"

"About ten years now. After high school, I got a two-year degree in criminal justice. I was planning to go into law enforcement, but a mutual friend introduced me to Shane McIntyre, my boss. He offered me a job, I accepted, and the rest is history."

"And you like your job. That's good. Not everyone can say that."

"I love it." His expression lights up. "I've met some great people, and I've made some really wonderful friends. I think you'd like them."

With a groan, Miguel puts his book aside and stands to stretch his arms and back. His T-shirt molds to his torso, accentuating his biceps and his flat abdomen. His shirt rides up a bit, and I get a peek at his lean waistline. I'm finding it hard to keep my eyes on my book.

He points to the rug. "Do you mind if I do some exercises? I'm getting stiff from inactivity."

"Go right ahead."

He drops down onto the floor and starts doing push-ups. I give up trying to read and watch his muscles tightening and flexing. Mentally, I count, but I give up sometime after fifty-nine. Good grief. I couldn't even do five push-ups to save my life.

When he finishes with the push-ups, he shifts position, bracing his feet underneath the sofa, and quickly powers through sit-ups. When he finally stops, he stands and says, "I wish I'd brought some weights. I'll have to call my buddy Jason and ask him to bring them to me." He nods toward the bathroom. "Do you mind if I go grab a quick shower?"

"Not at all."

Miguel grabs his duffle bag and disappears into the bathroom, and a minute later I hear the shower running. I try not to think about the fact that he's *naked* in there, with hot water streaming down his body.

Suddenly, I'm distracted by a faint scratching sound coming from somewhere close. At first, I think it might be Pumpkin using his scratching pad, but then I realize it's coming from *outside* the apartment.

Immediately, my pulse starts racing. I put my book down and walk quietly to the door so I can peer out the peephole, but I don't see anything. That doesn't mean much since visibility through the hole is so limited. Pumpkin joins me, sniffing along the door jamb.

The scratching intensifies, slow and insidious, sending a shudder through me. I picture long, sharp nails clawing my door. Miguel's still in the shower, though, as I can hear the water running. I consider going in there to tell him what's happening, but I don't want to invade his privacy.

Crap. It's just my luck that something happens when Miguel's otherwise occupied.

The scratching stops abruptly, and I listen intently. I peer out the peephole again, but I see nothing.

Without warning, there's a sharp thud on my door and the scratching resumes frantically. Pumpkin races off down the hallway and disappears into my bedroom. I turn my attention back to the sounds coming from outside my apartment. I picture roadkill coming to life and clawing at my door. I suppose it's possible if it's not quite dead yet. I shudder in horror as my imagination gets the better of me.

"Stop it!" I yell in frustration. I beat my fist against the door in an effort to scare it away. "Just stop!"

When I hear someone pounding back on the other side of the door, I stumble backward with a sharp cry and fall on my butt.

The shower shuts off abruptly. "Ruby?" A moment later, Miguel rushes into the living room in nothing but a bath towel wrapped around his waist. Water beads on his bare skin, and his hair is dripping wet.

"What is it?" he asks. He glances down at me. "Are you okay?" He grabs my hand and pulls me to my feet.

"Someone was scratching on the door," I say breathlessly. "I pounded on the door and told him to stop, and then he started pounding."

Miguel walks to the door and peers through the peephole. "Did you see anything?"

"No."

"Damn it! I need cameras in the hallway."

I find myself staring as water from his wet hair drips onto his broad shoulders before running down his muscled chest. *Good grief.* I didn't know a man could look like that.

Miguel releases the first deadbolt. "Ruby, go to your

room and lock the door."

My voice rises to a half-hysterical pitch. "You're opening the door?"

"Yes. Go."

I step back well out of the way, but I don't leave the room. I'm not leaving him to deal with this alone.

Miguel unlocks the door and opens it, but there's no one there. He steps out half-naked and scans the hallway in both directions before coming back inside and locking the door. "Whoever he is, he's long gone. Next time, call me as soon as you hear something, okay?"

I nod, thinking once again I have nothing to show for my claims, nothing but empty words. "I will."

* * *

That night, my mind races as I lie in bed, reliving that awful scratching sound coming from outside my apartment door. It was creepy and nerve-wracking. In the dark of night, I keep picturing horrible creatures with long claws. I think maybe I'm losing it.

It's windy tonight, and every time my window rattles, I flinch.

Pumpkin gets up and comes closer so he can lay his

head on my shoulder.

"Do you want to snuggle, sweet boy?" I ask as I stroke his back.

Ping.

I freeze, and my pulse kicks into high gear. I can't tell if I really heard that or if I imagined it. When Pumpkin jumps off the bed and scurries underneath, I know it's not my imagination.

Ping.

Another pebble hits my window. *It's him.*

Ping.

And another. *Oh, my God, it's really happening.*

Ping.

Ping.

I jump out of bed and race to the living room where I find Miguel lying on the sofa, reading. He's wearing a pair of gray sweats, and his feet and chest are bare. *Oh, wow.* All that smooth, warm brown skin.

He lays his book down. "Ruby? What's wrong?"

I point to my bedroom. "He's throwing pebbles at my window."

Miguel shoots to his feet. Immediately, my gaze fixes on the thin line of dark hair that bisects his lower abdomen, eventually disappearing beneath the waistband of his sweatpants.

I follow him to my bedroom. He heads straight for the window and stops to listen.

My heart is pounding so hard I'm sure he can hear it.

One minute passes, then another, and there's nothing but silence.

I'm starting to feel foolish, fearing I called him in here for nothing. "I swear I heard it," I whisper.

He raises his hand. "Wait."

And we wait some more.

Ping. Ping. Ping.

"There!" I cry. "That's it. That's him."

Miguel rushes out of my bedroom.

I race after him. "What are you doing?"

He pulls on a black T-shirt and shoves his feet into a pair of white sneakers. I watch in shock when he pulls a holstered black handgun out of his duffle bag and straps it to his chest.

He unlocks the door. "Lock up behind me."

Panic threatens to overwhelm me as he steps out into the hallway. I grab his forearm and try to pull him back inside. "You can't go out there!"

He glances down at me. "Ruby, this is why I'm here—to verify your claims. And this is how I do it—I catch him in the act."

"Please don't go out there. It's the middle of the night. It's dark outside. Let's just call the police and let them handle it."

"By the time the cops get here, he'll be long gone." His expression softens. "Ruby, this is my job. I know what I'm doing."

I tighten my grip on his forearm. "If something happens to you—"

He frowns. "Honey, I have to go." And then he gently pries my fingers free and walks away.

Immediately, I shut and lock the door. Then I run back to my bedroom and peer out my window. The parking lot is mostly dark, lit only by two light poles. I scan the lot, looking for movement, but I don't see anything until Miguel emerges from the building's rear exit almost directly beneath my window. I watch as he makes his way into the sea of cars, searching.

He's not going to find anything—I just know it.

After searching the lot, he comes back into the building. A few minutes later, there's a quiet knock on my door. "Ruby, it's me, Miguel."

I let him in. He locks the door before he crosses the room, removes his chest holster, and returns it to his duffle bag. "I'm sorry, but I didn't see anyone. I must have just missed him."

"It's okay. I'm just glad you didn't get hurt. I can't deal with anyone else getting hurt because of me."

He gently takes hold of my hands. "Ruby, what happened to your mother was a horrible tragedy, but it wasn't your fault."

Without warning, my eyes flood with tears. "It was."

Miguel sighs. "Sweetheart, no."

When he pulls me into his arms, I stiffen. I'm not used to being held like this. He loosens his hold, but he doesn't release me. His hand strokes the back of my head, like he's gentling a frightened animal. Gradually, I allow myself to relax.

"It wasn't your fault," he murmurs. "It was a random act of violence. You couldn't have known that would happen or prevented it." He releases me and holds me at arm's length so he can look me in the eyes. "You need to let go of this guilt."

I pull free and use my sleeves to dry my cheeks. "Lots of people have told me it wasn't my fault—therapists, teachers, Edward—but that doesn't change the facts. We were out shopping for *me*."

"That still doesn't make it your fault. Do you think

your mother would want you to go through life blaming yourself for her death? Would she want that?"

My chest tightens. "No."

"Don't you think it's time to let this go?"

Tears burn my eyes. "It's not that easy."

"I know."

I'm stunned by a mix of compassion and sorrow in his gaze.

I stare up at him. "You heard the pebbles hit my window tonight, right?" I know he did, but I need to hear him say it. I need confirmation that I'm not the only one hearing these things.

He nods. "I did."

"So you believe me?"

"Yes, I do."

Relief floods me. "Thank you."

"You don't need to thank me, Ruby. This is why I'm here. Now I just need to catch the bastard." He glances at the clock on the wall. It's nearly midnight. "Do you think you can sleep?"

"I'll try."

Miguel walks me to my bedroom and watches from the doorway as I climb back into bed. "Call if you hear anything else—or if you need me." And then he heads back to his own bed.

Pumpkin comes out from beneath the bed and joins me, trilling as he curls up beside me.

I scratch behind his ears. "He believes me, Pumpkin."

I drift off to sleep feeling safer and more secure than I have in a long time.

11

Miguel

I don't get much sleep that night. I lie awake for hours wondering if the asshat is going to throw more rocks at Ruby's window. If he does, I'm going to nail him. What kind of loser throws rocks at a girl's window in the middle of the night for the purpose of scaring her?

I wish I'd been able to grab him last night in the parking lot. If I had, this assignment would be over almost as soon as it began. Ruby would probably be relieved to get me out of her apartment. As for me—I guess I'd be glad to give Ruby some answers and put an end to her torment. I'd move on to my next assignment, of course. But I'd be disappointed that I didn't get a chance to know her better.

I check my watch—it's six-thirty. Normally, I'd get up about now and put in a quick workout in my apartment, but I can't do that here. No equipment. If it looks like I'm going to be here a while, I should ask Ruby if she'd mind me bringing some free weights over.

I'm still lying on the sofa when I hear a muted thud coming from outside the apartment door. I get up and walk to the door so I can peer out the peephole. I see nothing. But I can't discount the sound I heard, so I turn off the security system, unlock the door, and open it just a few inches with the chain still in place.

On the welcome mat below is one of those cheap plastic shopping bags, filthy and dripping wet. That sure as hell wasn't there last night when I returned from my reconnaissance out in the parking lot.

I release the chain and step out into the hallway and look left and right. There's no one out here.

Then I look down at that damn plastic bag. I've got a bad feeling about this. A really bad feeling. Crouching, I pinch the end of one of the bag's handles between my index finger and thumb and carefully lift. Putrid air wafts up into my face and just as I feared, there's something dead in the bag. From the little I can see, it looks like roadkill—a raccoon. It's old roadkill. The carcass is already mostly decomposed. I consider saving the bag and its contents, but the chance of getting any meaningful forensic evidence out of this mess is low.

I hear a soft gasp behind me and look back to see Ruby peering outside her apartment from several feet back from the door.

"There's something dead in that bag, isn't there?" she asks.

I nod. "Roadkill. Looks like a raccoon."

She steps back. "I'll grab a trash bag. Would you mind throwing it down the trash chute?" She points toward the end of the hall.

"Sure. Just let me take a couple of pics." When I pull my phone out of my back pocket, she disappears from sight.

She brings me a heavy duty black trash bag, and I bag it up. After I dispose of the bag down the chute, I head back into the apartment and lock the door behind me. I find Ruby in the kitchen making coffee.

"I'll call my boss and let him know about the rock

throwing and the package left at your door. What about your dad? Do you want me to call him with an update?"

Ruby's expression tightens and she shakes her head. "He'll just say I planted it."

"I can vouch for the fact that you didn't. There's no way you could have put that there." For one thing, she couldn't have snuck past me in the night to open the door. And obviously, she couldn't have gone outside to pick up a dead raccoon off the street.

"My father thinks I'm making this up. Nothing we say will change his mind." She opens the fridge door, closes it, then opens the freezer. "How about waffles today? I feel like having something different."

"Sure. That sounds great. Can I help?"

"That's okay. I've got it."

I end up sitting at the little kitchen table with my coffee and keeping her company while she toasts the waffles. When the food's almost ready, I look in the fridge for the maple syrup and hold up the bottle to her. "We have enough for this morning, but you're about out of syrup."

"We can't have that," she says with a laugh. "I need my syrup." When the waffles are ready, she says, "Butter's on the counter." She points at a covered white ceramic dish.

"I'm getting low on eggs and bread, too. I'm not used to feeding two. I'll have to place a grocery order soon. If there's anything specific you want, just let me know, and I'll add it to the list."

Before she sits down to eat, Ruby puts Pumpkin's food in his bowl and sets it on the floor. He literally pounces on the food, scarfing it up like he's starving.

"Are you sure you're feeding him enough?" I ask, laughing.

"He always eats like it's his last meal," Ruby says. "He was a stray kitten when I got him. He has food scarcity issues."

"How did you end up with a stray kitten in the first place?"

"It was Darren's doing actually. He found Pumpkin in the parking lot one morning, hiding underneath his car. The kitten had clearly been on his own for a while. He was filthy. His fur was matted, he had infections in both eyes, and he was skin and bones. Darren brought him up to me. He said he thought I could use a friend. He was right. I found a vet who did house calls. The rest is history."

After we eat, I help with clearing the table and washing the dishes. I wash this time, Ruby dries.

"Mind if I grab a quick shower?" I ask her when we're done.

"Go right ahead."

I grab my toiletries from my kit and a change of clothes and head to the bathroom. Despite being outdated—with its pink tiles on the wall and white steel tub—it's clean and uncluttered. I strip off my PJ bottoms and T-shirt and step beneath the hot spray. Five minutes later, I'm out of the shower, after a quick scrub and a hair wash. I dress quickly in jeans and a T-shirt.

When I return to the living room, I find Ruby seated in the armchair, looking at her phone. "Everything okay?" I ask her.

She nods. "I'm reading."

It's a little after eight o'clock, so I figure Shane's in the office by now. I call him with an update.

"Miguel, how's it going?" he asks as he answers my call. "Jake tells me the security system has been installed."

"Yes, thanks. We had a couple of interesting developments overnight."

"Such as?"

I tell him all about the rock throwing last night and the roadkill on her welcome mat this morning. "Someone's definitely terrorizing Ruby."

"I see. I'll call Edward and give him an update. Keep me posted on any further developments."

"Got it. Thanks."

As soon as I end the call, Ruby asks, "Do you think he believed you?" She sounds a bit skeptical.

"Of course."

She frowns. "My turn to get ready, and then I need to get to work." After she gets dressed, Ruby disappears into her art studio.

At ten, there's a loud knock on the door. I peer through the peephole to see a very pissed off older guy standing there. "Ruby? Someone's at the door."

The man knocks again, this time harder. "Ruby, open the damn door, right this minute!"

I turn as Ruby enters the room. She rolls her eyes. "That's my father."

"Should I let him in?"

Looking resigned, she nods. "Might as well. He won't go away until we do. He'll just get louder and more obnoxious the longer he waits."

I open the door. "Mr. Foster, come in."

The man glares as he brushes past me. "Who the hell are you?"

"Dad!" Ruby cries. "Don't speak to Miguel like that."

Allen Foster ignores his daughter. "I asked you a question, son. Who the hell are you?"

"Miguel Rodriguez, sir," I say, hoping to keep things civil for Ruby's sake. "I was hired to find out who's terrorizing your daughter."

"Don't be ridiculous," Foster says. "She's making it up for attention." He eyes me from head to toe. "Hired? Who hired you? I sure as hell didn't, and Ruby can't afford to hire security."

"Edward did," Ruby says.

At the mention of Edward McCall's name, Allen Foster's expression darkens. "What the hell? He had no right to do that." Foster turns his attention back to me. "Where are you from?" he asks me.

"He's from McIntyre Security," Ruby says, completely misunderstanding the nature of his question.

I know what he's getting at. I've heard this question a million times. "Chicago."

"No, I mean where were you born?"

"Cook County Hospital."

Foster's frown deepens and he practically growls. "Don't play stupid with me, son. You know exactly what I mean."

Yeah, I do. "My grandparents emigrated to Chicago

from Mexico City back in the sixties. Both of my grandfathers were structural engineers who came here on employment visas during a construction boom. Both of my parents were born in Chicago. I'm the oldest of eight kids, all born and raised right here in the Windy City."

When Ruby steps between me and her father, my heart melts. It's sweet of her to want to protect me from her father's prejudice, but completely unnecessary. I've heard and experienced far worse. "Ruby, it's okay."

"No, it's not." She points to the door. "Dad, I think you should leave."

Foster scowls at his daughter. "After everything I've done for you, you ungrateful little—"

Now it's my turn to step in. "Mr. Foster, Ruby asked you to leave. I think you should do as she asks."

He turns his scowl on me. "And if I don't?"

"Then I'll make you."

Ruby makes a sound of exasperation. "Dad, why are you here?"

"Edward called to tell me he'd hired security. I wanted to see for myself." He gives me a disapproving look. "I don't think it's appropriate for a strange man to be staying in my daughter's apartment."

"It's fine, Dad," Ruby says.

Foster ignores Ruby and glares at me. "Get your stuff and get out—now!"

This is escalating quickly. "Mr. Foster—"

"No, don't you *Mr. Foster* me. Edward had no right to go behind my back. *I'm* Ruby's father, and I'll decide what's best for her. I'm telling you to get out. Your services are no longer needed." He glances at the neatly folded bedding and the pillow piled at one end of the sofa and sneers. "Frankly, I think it's unseemly for you to be staying here."

"You can't fire Miguel," Ruby says. "You aren't the one who hired him."

Foster turns to his daughter, clearly aggravated. "If you're so worried about your safety, then come back home where you belong."

She shakes her head. "I told you I'm not moving back home."

"Mr. Foster," I say, hoping to redirect the conversation. "Someone *is* terrorizing Ruby."

"You have proof?" he asks me, clearly skeptical.

"Yes."

"You listen to me, young lady," Foster says, directing his comments back to Ruby. "This guy is feeding right into your paranoia. It's job security for him if he convinces you you're in danger."

I glance at Ruby and find her eyes on me, wide and uncertain. She's scared. She's afraid I'm going to up and leave her here to deal with this alone. I give her a subtle shake of my head, and she relaxes.

"You should go now," Ruby tells her father. "I don't want to hear any more."

Fuming, Foster opens the door and walks out, slamming it behind him. Ruby rushes forward to lock it. She turns to face me, watching me expectantly.

"I'm not leaving you, Ruby."

She gives me a relieved smile, but then her lips flatten, and she swallows hard. "I want to apologize for the things my father said to you. He has a tendency to be suspicious of anyone who looks a certain way." Her arms cross over her chest, and she's practically hugging herself. She's afraid, and she feels alone.

I step forward and hold out my arms to her, giving her the choice to accept comfort from me or not. She hesitates for only a split second before she walks into my arms. As I run a hand up and down her back, I can feel her trembling. "You have nothing to apologize for, Ruby. I hear stuff like that all the time. It means nothing. And you're definitely not responsible for anything your father says."

She slips her arms around my waist and hugs me back. "I'm so sorry about all of this." Her voice is muffled against my shirt. "This isn't your problem. *I'm* not your problem. I wouldn't blame you if you decided to leave."

I tighten my hold on her. "I'm not abandoning you, Ruby."

After Ruby returns to her work, I call Shane back to give him a heads up about Foster's visit, just in case the man tries to cause trouble for Shane.

Shane sighs. "Don't worry about Foster. If he causes problems, I'll have a talk with him. In the meantime, keep doing what you're doing. We'll get to the bottom of this and make sure Ruby's safe."

After we end the call, I walk down the hall to Ruby's studio and poke my head through the open doorway. "You doing okay?"

She turns in her chair to face me. "Yeah. I just feel crappy for the things my dad said to you."

"I mean it, you don't need to apologize." I come into the room and check out the painting of a calico cat and compare it to the photograph clipped to her easel. "How do you do that? You've got a real gift."

When she smiles, tiny dimples appear. "Thanks. I appreciate the compliment."

"I came to ask if you like enchiladas."

She lights up. "I love them. Why?"

"Because I want to make you dinner tonight. How about it?"

Her smile deepens. "I would love that. But we'll need some ingredients. I probably don't have a lot of what you'd need." She hands me the notepad on her worktable. It's a grocery list already in progress.

Eggs

Milk

Bread

Cheese

Toilet paper

Bananas

Apples

Avocados

Syrup

"Add whatever you need for the enchiladas to the list," she says, "and anything else you want. I'll place an order later this morning, and we'll have it in time for dinner."

I glance down once more at the tiny painting she's working on. "I'd like to commission you for a painting."

"Really? What would you like me to paint?"

"My grandma's dog, Sugar. She's a tiny long-haired Chihuahua—so small she fits in the palm of my hand. She's the sweetest little dog I've ever known. She's *mi abuelita's* baby."

"I'd be happy to. I just need a good photo of the dog."

I pull out my phone and scroll through my camera roll until I find a good photo of Sugar.

Ruby studies the photo. "That is one seriously cute dog."

"Can you do it?"

She nods. "Yes, absolutely. I'll fit it into my queue."

"Perfect. My grandma's birthday is coming up. This would be the perfect gift."

After I add the ingredients I'll need for dinner to the list, Ruby places the order.

"We'll have it by four o'clock," she says. "Will you teach me to make enchiladas?"

"Of course, but if you want to learn from the best, you should let my grandma teach you."

Ruby's smile quickly falls, and immediately I wish I'd kept my mouth shut. She'd have to leave her apartment to meet my family, and that's obviously not going to happen. "Ruby, I'm sorry. I wasn't thinking."

She shakes it off. "No, it's fine." She nods toward the

painting she's working on. "I'd better get back to this. I'd like to finish it today."

"Sure." I motion toward the living room. "I'll let you work now."

It occurs to me that, if I can't bring Ruby to my grandma's house, maybe I can bring my grandma to Ruby. Ruby seems fine having me here. I think she might be open to having visitors. Maybe I could get one of my female friends to come over. They're all around Ruby's age, and they've all dealt with serious traumas. If Ruby won't go out into the world, maybe I can bring a little bit of the world here to her.

12

Ruby

In the middle of the afternoon, we get a visitor—Miguel's boss.

Miguel lets him in while I watch from down the hall from my studio doorway. Miguel warned me that Mr. McIntyre was coming so I wouldn't be caught off guard. I suspect the man's here to talk about my father's visit.

Shane McIntyre is a good-looking man, in his late thirties, I'd guess. He's tall with short brown hair and a trim beard. His eyes are a surprisingly bright shade of blue. He definitely looks the CEO type, dressed in a dark gray suit with a white dress shirt and a matching gray tie.

He nods to me, giving me a warm, friendly smile. "Hello, Ms. Foster. It's a pleasure to meet you."

"Hi." I look from Shane to Miguel, who are standing side by side. "I'm sorry my father was so rude to Miguel this morning. I think he sees everyone as a servant he can boss around. I assure you it was nothing personal against Miguel. He's been wonderful."

Shane gently elbows Miguel. "That's why I chose him for your case." The man smiles again, and it's clear he's making an effort to put me at ease. "Miguel was once my wife's bodyguard—before she was my wife." He chuckles. "Before I even met her, in fact. So, yes, I know how wonderful he is. My wife reminds me of this all the time."

Shane winks at Miguel, who elbows his boss right back. It's clear the two men have a good relationship.

"Stop," Miguel says to his boss. "You're going to make me blush."

Shane laughs, and then addresses me once more. "Miguel's caught me up to date on the events that have occurred since he arrived. We'll catch your stalker soon."

Feeling more at ease, I come forward and join them

in the living room. "I appreciate your support, Mr. McIntyre."

"Please, call me Shane."

I notice Shane is careful to keep his distance. He doesn't offer to shake my hand, which I appreciate. "Well, I'll be going now," he says. "I just wanted to stop by, say hello, and assure you that we won't let your father's reaction derail our investigation."

Miguel's boss lets himself out—without making any comments about the number of locks on my door—and Miguel secures the door after he's gone. I don't even have to ask him to do it. He just knows.

Miguel turns to face me, and for a moment we just look at each other. I'm struck yet again by how handsome he is. I'm struck by the fact that he doesn't seem to possess an ounce of vanity, even though he'd have every right to.

And then it dawns on me. I've never considered the fact that surely he has someone special in his life. Someone that amazing would have to, and yet he's stuck here with me twenty-four-seven. That's not fair to him or to his partner. "If you need to leave for a while, go do something, or go see someone, it's totally fine, you know."

He looks confused. "I don't need to go anywhere."

"Don't you have someone—like a girlfriend or, you know, *someone*—to go home to?"

He laughs. "Oh, no. There's no one."

I find that hard to believe. This guy must have women throwing themselves at him all the time. "There's no one?" How's that even possible? He's—well, he's pretty amazing.

Smiling, he shakes his head. "I have friends, yes. Lots of them. But I'm not dating anyone, if that's what you mean. I work long hours. I don't have time to meet women." He laughs. "It's a common problem in my line of work. We hardly get any free time. Several of my friends ended up falling in love with their clients, and now we joke that McIntyre Security is actually a dating service in disguise."

"Your friends fell in love with their clients? Is that allowed?"

"Well, Shane can hardly get on his people for doing it when he did it himself. He fell in love with one of his clients, Beth, and married her. They have two young children now." He looks thoughtful. "Speaking of my friends, I was wondering if I could invite a couple of them over for a visit. I thought you might like to meet another young woman your age. What do you say?"

The air leaves my lungs in a rush, and I feel lightheaded. "I don't know. I'm not sure how I'd feel about having more strangers in my apartment."

"You're doing fine with me here, and I'm a stranger. Or at least I was. I'm not a stranger anymore, am I?"

"That's different. You're—" Before I can say another word, there's a knock at the door. I automatically flinch.

"Miss Ruby," says a muffled voice through the door. "It's me, Leo. I'm here with your groceries."

I start toward the door, but Miguel says, "I'll get it."

Miguel's already walking to the door and peering out the peephole. Then he unlocks the door, opens it, and there's Leo from Frank's Market, holding two paper sacks of groceries in his arms.

Leo's eyes widen in surprise when he sees Miguel, probably because he's not used to seeing someone else in my apartment. He glances past Miguel until his gaze lands on me. "Miss Ruby, is everything okay?"

"Yes, fine," I say.

Miguel takes the bags from Leo, who's staring at him.

"It's okay. Miguel's a friend," I tell him, hoping to reassure him that everything's all right.

Leo finally breaks his stare and leaves. Miguel closes the door. I lock it as he carries the bags of groceries to the kitchen.

"Perfect timing on the groceries, right?" I say. "Now you can teach me to make authentic Mexican enchiladas."

While Miguel empties the bags, I put the items where they go. In addition to the staples I ordered, I find corn tortillas, sweet corn, several varieties of dried chiles, as well as onions, garlic, tomatoes, cilantro, and a lime. The one thing I don't see is a can of enchilada sauce.

"You're making the sauce from scratch?" I ask, surprised.

He nods. "Of course. My grandma would box my ears if she found out I used canned enchilada sauce." He turns on the faucet and washes his hands. "Now, watch and learn."

Pumpkin hovers at my feet, meowing plaintively.

"I think someone's hungry," Miguel says, nodding at the cat.

I grab his bowl, dish out his dinner, and set it on the floor. As usual, he pounces on it.

I pull up a stool so I can watch Miguel make enchilada sauce. It's quite a production as he toasts several different types of dried peppers in a skillet. After he sets those aside, he toasts tomatoes, garlic, and onions.

My stomach is already growling. "This is going to take

a while, isn't it?"

He grins at me. "Are you hungry?"

I nod guiltily. "Yeah."

Smiling, he grabs a bowl and dumps in some tortilla chips. "Here, snack on these. This should tide you over until dinner is ready."

After preparing the peppers, he soaks them in boiling water to soften them. After half an hour of soak time, he adds the softened peppers, tomatoes, onions, and garlic to a blender and purees them. He puts the pureed sauce in a pot, adds some oregano and ground cumin, and puts the pot on the stove to simmer.

While the sauce simmers, he cooks some ground beef with onions and garlic, mixing it with shredded Mexican cheeses before rolling the ingredients into the corn tortillas. Finally, he lays the enchiladas in a baking dish and pours the sauce over the top. "It won't be much longer now," he says.

"You make that look so easy," I say, shaking my head in amazement. "From now on, you're in charge of cooking. I don't think my kitchen has ever smelled this good."

He laughs, clearly pleased by my reaction. "This is nothing. You should try my grandma's cooking. Have you ever been to a Mexican restaurant—an authentic one?"

I nod. "A few times, when I was a kid. My parents loved trying different cuisines. I'm afraid I was probably too young to appreciate it."

"My uncle and his family own a restaurant. I used to work there in the summers with my cousins. Their food's amazing—you should try their tacos al pastor. Or the tacos carne asada. They're so good. I'd love to take you there."

My smile falls as my heart starts hammering against my ribs. I shake my head. "I'm sorry, but I can't."

He winces. "Ruby, I'm sorry. I wasn't thinking. I didn't mean to—"

"It's okay, really." I hop down from my stool. "I think I'll go work on my painting until dinner's ready. It looks like you've got everything under control."

He watches me walk away. "I'll call you when it's time to eat."

Dinner is absolutely delicious, of course. No surprise there. The enchiladas are flavorful and tender, practically melting in my mouth. "Mmm, I think your grandmother would be proud of you."

Miguel smiles as he chews. After he swallows, he says, "I'm glad you like them."

After we finish eating, we clean up the kitchen together. We seem to have developed a comfortable routine. I'm not used to having help. It's nice.

"How about ice cream for dessert?" he asks.

We dish up two bowls of mint chocolate chip ice cream and get comfortable on the sofa. Pumpkin curls up between us.

Miguel picks up the remote and skims through the offerings on Netflix.

"The new season of *Stranger Things* just dropped. Do you want to watch it?"

"That's the show with the kids and the creepy stuff in the upside down? Sure."

He smiles. "Yeah, that's the one."

13

Miguel

We're seated side-by-side on the sofa, with our feet propped on the coffee table, eating our ice cream, when there's a knock at the door.

Ruby jumps.

"It's okay. I'll get it," I say. I pause the show and walk to the door so I can look through the peephole. I'm surprised to see who's here. Since I started picking up Ruby's mail and taking out her trash, we haven't seen Darren. "It's Darren. Do you want me to open the door?"

Ruby looks surprised. "Yeah."

I unlock the door and open it a foot or so. Darren ignores me and peers through the opening. "Ruby? Can I talk to you?"

The guy's tenacious, I'll give him that. I don't think he likes the fact that I'm encroaching on his territory.

Ruby joins me at the door. "Hi, Darren? What is it?"

Darren glowers at me. "Do you mind not eavesdropping on our conversation?"

Well, yeah. I do mind.

Before I can respond, Ruby nods to me. "It's okay, Miguel."

I take a few steps back, out of his sight, but close enough to monitor their conversation.

Darren lowers his voice to a whisper. "Ruby, I don't like this guy being in your apartment. How well do you know him?"

"I know him well enough," she says, sounding more than a little defensive.

Darren tries a different tack. "How long have you known him?"

"Just a couple of days, but it's not what you think."

"Oh, I think I know how it is," Darren whispers. "You

need to get rid of him, Ruby. He's not *safe*." Darren emphasizes the word *safe*. He sure knows how to prey on Ruby's fears. "He's a *stranger*. There's no telling what he might do."

"I'm fine, Darren," she tells him. "You don't need to worry. I have to go now. We're watching something."

Giving him an apologetic smile, Ruby slowly closes the door. At the last second, I catch a glimpse of his expression—he's pissed.

"I'm sure you heard that," Ruby says, looking apologetic. "I'm sure he didn't mean that." Ruby locks the door.

We return to the sofa and resume the show. It sure seems like a lot of people are miffed at the idea of me staying here with Ruby. I keep replaying every manipulative thing Darren said to Ruby and try to decide if he's a real risk to her or just a jealous suitor who sees my presence in her apartment as a threat.

I'm hyperaware of Ruby's presence beside me—just inches away. Long strands of her fiery red hair hang loose over her shoulder and down her back. I find myself wanting to reach out and touch the strands to see if they're as silky as they look. She smells like roses. I don't know if it's from perfume or the scent of her soap or shampoo.

The longer I sit this close to her, the guiltier I feel. It's wrong on so many levels for me to be attracted to her. I'm here as her protector, for fuck's sake. I have no business moving in on her personal space.

Maybe I shouldn't be so hasty to blame Darren for his concern. The truth is—I do think about Ruby in ways I shouldn't. I'd never act on it—it would be blatantly unprofessional. And yet, as we're sitting here together, so close that our arms almost touch, I'm aware of her every movement, every shift of her body, every sigh she makes.

We're into the second episode now, and neither one of us seems ready to call it quits. When the current episode ends, Ruby gathers up our empty ice cream bowls and spoons and takes them to the kitchen. Pumpkin follows her, probably in case he might get a second dinner.

This time, I don't follow her. I don't offer to help. I think maybe it's best if there's a little space between us.

When she's done in the kitchen, she switches off the light and returns to the living room. "It's getting late, so I think I'll head to bed now. Goodnight, Miguel. Thank you for a delicious dinner and for, well, everything."

"My pleasure."

I watch her walk away, already feeling the loss of her presence. "Goodnight, Ruby. Sleep well."

She spends a few minutes in the bathroom before she disappears into her bedroom and shuts the door.

I get myself ready for bed and set the security alarm before making up my bed on the sofa. I lie down with my book and resume reading.

It's just after midnight when I hear glass shatter. I jump up from the sofa and race down the hallway to Ruby's bedroom. The door flies open just as I reach it.

Ruby's standing there, her face flushed. She's breathing hard as she holds up a rock the size of her fist. "It came right through the window!"

I swallow a curse and run to get my shoes and shirt on. I strap my gun holster to my chest, turn off the security system, and unlock the door. "Lock this behind me," I say as I exit the apartment.

"Miguel, be careful!" she calls after me.

As I'm racing to the stairwell, Darren's apartment door opens and he steps out into the hall. He's in his pajamas, his hair mussed from sleep. He's blinking against the bright hallway lights. "Did you hear that? What's going on?"

"Ruby, lock your door!" I yell back at her, seeing that her door's still open.

Darren looks genuinely worried. "Is Ruby okay?"

"Now, Ruby!" I don't want Darren talking to her, and I can't waste another second giving her instructions. I hear Ruby's door close as I'm jogging down the staircase. I race out the back door into the parking lot just in time to see a figure dressed in a dark hoodie racing away from the building. I take off after him, determined to catch him this time.

He weaves through the cars as he heads for the park. I stay on his trail, gaining on him with each passing second. I lunge at him, taking him to the ground, and wrap my arms and legs around him, holding him immobile.

"What the fuck?" the guy yells as he fights my hold. He thrashes violently, trying to head-butt me. "Let me go, you moron." He sounds young.

I roll us so that I'm sitting on him. After yanking the hood off his head, then a black knit cap, I stare down into a frightened teenage boy's face. His brown eyes are huge, and he's white as a ghost. He can't be more than sixteen. "Who the fuck are you?" I demand.

He glares up at me as he struggles to break free.

I grab a fistful of his sweatshirt and shake him. "I asked you a question. Who are you?"

"Aaron," he says, breathing hard.

"Why were you throwing rocks at that apartment

window?"

"I don't know!" he cries. "Some guy paid me fifty bucks to do it. He said it would be funny. It was supposed to be a prank."

"What guy?"

"I don't know. Just some dude. He's old, like even older than you."

"Describe him."

"I didn't really see much. It was dark out."

"Was he dark or fair?"

"He was a white guy. That's all I know."

"Did he have dark hair or light?"

The kid shrugs. "I couldn't tell. He was wearing a hat, and like I said, man, it was dark out."

"When did he hire you?"

"Tonight. About an hour ago. I was walking down the street, and he called me over, gave me fifty bucks to throw rocks at a window."

"Did he tell you exactly which window to hit?"

"Yeah. He told me to go to the back of the building, count over six windows from the left on the second floor. Hey, man, I'm sorry. He said it would be funny. You're not gonna call the cops, are you?"

I let go of the kid's shirt and stand. "Get up."

He jumps to his feet and brushes off his clothes. "Look, I'm sorry, but it was fifty bucks, you know? That's a lot of money."

I pull one of my cards out of my back pocket and hand it to the kid. "If you see him again, you call me, all right? And if you ever throw a rock—or anything else for that matter—at that apartment, I will rip you a new one, you got it?"

"Yeah, man. I got it. Sheesh."

"If there's a next time, I'm callin' the cops. Understand?"

"Yeah, I hear you." Then the kid takes off running across the park, quickly disappearing into the trees.

When I return to the apartment, I'm sorry that I don't have more information to share with Ruby, but I'm pretty sure that kid doesn't present any real threat to Ruby. I believed him when he said he was paid to throw the rock at her window.

I knock on Ruby's apartment door. "Ruby, it's me."

She opens the door, looking exhausted and scared. "Did you catch him?"

I nod. "It was just a kid—a teenager. He said someone hired him to throw rocks at your window." I come inside and lock the door. "He couldn't tell me who hired him."

Ruby's shoulders fall. "What am I going to do about

the window?"

"We can call Rick in the morning. Hopefully he can repair it quickly."

Ruby glances down the hall toward her bedroom, indecision marring her expression. I think she's afraid to sleep in her bedroom.

"Do you want to sleep on the sofa?" I ask.

She shakes her head. "I can't take your bed. Where will you sleep?"

"I'll sleep on the floor. It's no problem."

"I have a sleeping bag," she says. "I'll take the floor."

I chuckle. "Honey, I'm not letting you sleep on the floor, and that's final, so don't even waste your breath arguing with me."

A smile flits across her face. "Then what are we going to do?"

"Well, how about this? You sleep in your own bed—"

Her eyes widen. "No! I don't feel safe in there. Not with a hole in the window."

"Wait. I'm not done. You sleep in your bed, and I'll sleep on the floor in your room. Will that help? Is there any glass on your bed?"

She shakes her head. "Just on the floor beneath the window."

"Okay then. Are you okay with this plan?"

She thinks for a minute, then nods. "Yes."

"All right, then. Let's go to bed." I set the security system, then walk Ruby to her bedroom. The heavy drapes are moving just a bit, courtesy of the wind blowing through the hole in her window, but it's not too bad.

I turn the light on and check the floor for glass. Fortunately, the glass is contained mostly beneath the window. "Have you got a broom and dustpan?" I ask.

She runs out of the bedroom, returning a couple minutes later with the items I asked for.

"Stay back," I tell her as I take the broom and dustpan from her.

"I can help," she offers.

"No, you're barefoot. Sit." I point to the bed.

Ruby climbs up onto the bed and watches me sweep up the shards. I dispose of the glass in the kitchen trash can.

"Now, where's that sleeping bag you said you have?"

"Wait! I can't let you sleep on the floor, not after everything you've done for me."

"Then what do you suggest we do?"

She hesitates a moment, then blurts out, "We can share the bed."

"Ruby." Something tells me this isn't a good idea. I know it's not a good idea for me. Sharing a bed? "Are you sure?"

She nods. "Yes."

14

Ruby

"I'm sorry," I say as we lie side by side on my bed in the dark. My heart is pounding, but it's not from fear. Yes, I was afraid to sleep alone in my bedroom knowing there was a hole in the window. But it's not fear that's making my pulse run away now. It's the knowledge that Miguel is in my bed. I know I shouldn't feel this way, but I can't help it. He's a real-life knight in shining armor. I've never met anyone like him before. *And he's in my bed!*

"You don't need to apologize to me, Ruby," he says

quietly. Miguel reaches over blindly in the dark and takes my hand, linking our fingers together. "Not ever."

I'm certain he's going to make some comment about just doing his job, but he doesn't, and I'm glad. He makes me feel safe, and that's something I haven't felt in years. I'd hate for him to trivialize it by saying he's just doing his job. I know it's his job, but for a little while I want to forget that and just enjoy his company.

"I'm sure there are other things you'd rather be doing," I say, unable to stop myself from stating the obvious. It's true. I know it is. I may have my share of problems, but I'm not delusional. I'm not going to kid myself into thinking he's here with me because he wants to be. He's being *paid* to protect me.

"Nope," he says lightly as he rubs his thumb along mine. "There's nowhere else I want to be right now."

My chest tightens, and I feel tears pricking at my eyes. I close my lids tightly to stave off tears. I'm not going to ruin the moment by crying. "Thank you for being here. For staying even after my dad was so rude to you. I'm grateful."

He squeezes my hand. "You don't need to thank me either. The door is locked, the security system is set, and you're safe, I promise. Just relax and try to sleep."

"Okay." I turn my face to him, but it's too dark for me to even see his profile. "Goodnight, Miguel."

He releases my hand. "Goodnight, Ruby."

I close my eyes and attempt to will myself to sleep, but no such luck. I'm far too aware of Miguel and the fact there's a man in my bed. Pumpkin has no such qualms. He jumps up on the bed with a chirp and nestles in between us, purring contentedly. I, on the other hand, am feeling way too self-conscious to relax.

What if I snore?

What if I talk in my sleep?

I close my eyes and pretend I'm asleep. Before long, I hear Miguel's deep, even breathing. It sounds nice. I turn over, facing away from him, and start counting sheep.

* * *

When I wake the next morning, Miguel is still asleep. He's lying on his back, and I'm pressed up against his side, my arm slung over his waist. My pulse starts tripping.

Ohmygod.

I freeze, hoping not to wake him.

This is so wrong, so inappropriate. And yet, I don't want it to end. I could lie here with him like this forever, just the two of us. I realize the drapes are open slightly, just enough to let in a bit of morning sunlight.

I steal a moment to study his profile, his warm golden-brown skin, his dark dark hair, black as night, the dark slash of his eyebrow, the line of his nose. His lips are relaxed in sleep, framed perfectly by his trim beard and mustache. He says he doesn't have a girlfriend, or anyone special, but if he did, I'd be so jealous.

He stirs, moaning softly as his chest rises on a deep breath. Then, to my utter shock, his left hand comes up and covers my hand. I know it's just a reflex because he's still half-asleep.

He inhales deeply, then yawns. "Good morning," he says, his voice rough from sleep.

I attempt to pull my arm back, but he catches my hand for a split second, then abruptly lets it go.

He turns on his side to face me. "How'd you sleep?"

"Pretty well, thanks to you."

Pumpkin jumps up on the bed, purring like a motorboat, and walks across Miguel's abdomen.

"Pumpkin, get off," I say, laughing as I push the cat off him.

"It's okay." Miguel laughs. "I grew up with a house full of pets." He reaches out to scratch Pumpkin's chin.

I slide off the foot of the bed.

Miguel sits up and surveys the floor. "Careful. Watch for broken glass." He watches me make my way carefully to the door. "So, what's on the agenda for today?"

"Pretty much the same as every day. Some painting, a little bit of reading, and maybe watch a movie. How about you?"

He smiles. "Pretty much the same. I do what you do, minus the painting part, and add in some exercise."

When I come out of the bathroom, I see him across the hall, sitting on the edge of my bed petting Pumpkin. "The bathroom's all yours," I say.

Then I get dressed in my bedroom. My gaze lands on the broken pane of glass, reminding me that I need to call Rick to tell him about the window. I hope he can fix it soon. *Oh, great, another person in my apartment.*

I'm in the kitchen making coffee when Miguel walks into the living room and grabs a change of clothes from his duffle bag.

"I need to do laundry today," he says. "I'm about out of clean clothes."

I point to the small utility closet next to the kitchen. "The washer's all yours. You know, you can hang up your clothes in my closet if you want, so they don't wrinkle."

"Thanks. That'd be great." He folds the bedding left on the sofa from last night and puts it away in the linen cupboard. "Can I ask a favor?"

I pour us each a cup of coffee. "Of course. Anything."

"Would you mind if I ask a friend to bring over a few things from my apartment? Namely my free weights."

My pulse skips a beat at the mention of someone coming over. But I can hardly say no after everything Miguel's done for me. "No, I don't mind."

"Thanks. I'll give him a call and see if they're available this afternoon."

"They?"

"Jason and his girlfriend, Layla. I'm sure he'll want to bring her along. They're pretty inseparable. It's okay if he brings Layla with him?"

I nod. "Sure. How about French toast for breakfast?" I ask. "With all the fixins—syrup, cinnamon, and whipped cream." I smile at the memory. "My mom made this for me for Sunday breakfast."

"That sounds perfect," he says as he grabs his phone and types in a text message. "Remind me to make you some cinnamon oatmeal sometime. That's what I loved as a kid."

A moment later, his phone chimes with a return message. "Perfect. Jason and Layla will come over this afternoon and bring me a few dumbbells."

My heart slams into my ribs. Two people. Two more strangers.

"Ruby? Is everything okay?"

I nod as I start gathering the ingredients to make breakfast. "Yes, fine."

"Can I help?"

"No, no, I'm fine." I point to his mug on the counter. "Your coffee's ready. Grab it while it's hot."

A moment later he's standing beside me, his presence looming. I can actually feel the heat from his body radiating in my direction. "What's wrong?" he asks. "Are you worried about Jason and Layla coming over? I can ask Jason to leave the dumbbells downstairs in the lobby. They don't have to come up."

"No, it's okay if they come up. Really, it's fine." It's not, but I don't want to begrudge him seeing his friends.

"Are you sure? I promise you they won't be offended if I ask them not to come up."

I start cracking eggs into a bowl. "I'm sure."

He leans closer, his firm bicep pressing against my shoulder. "I think you'll really like Layla," he says in a quiet voice. "You two have a lot in common."

That certainly piques my curiosity. "Like what?"

"Let's just say, you both have dealt with trauma. Who knows? Maybe you two could become friends."

He's still leaning close, and I think I must be imagining it when I feel his breath ruffle my hair. "We can never have too many friends."

A shiver travels down my spine. The realization that I'm already so used to having him here scares me. But what scares me most is how I'll handle his absence when he leaves. Because he's going to leave eventually. And then I'll be alone once more.

After we finish breakfast, I call the office to let Rick know about the broken window. As expected, he's not happy about the news.

"Fine," he says. "I probably have some panes of glass lying around in storage I can use to replace the broken one. I'll be up in a little bit to fix it."

An hour later, there's a knock at the door. Miguel answers it, opening the door to let Rick in. He's got tools and a pane of glass with him.

"Which window?" he asks. He sounds irritated.

"The first bedroom," I say, pointing. "Someone threw a rock through my window last night."

Rick glances at Miguel. "Where were you when this

happened?"

"Right here in the apartment," Miguel says. "Why? You think I did it?"

Rick grunts as he heads to my bedroom. "Wouldn't put it past you," he mumbles.

Miguel and I watch from the bedroom doorway as Rick replaces the broken pane and reseals it.

When he's done, he gathers up his tools and the broken pane, then brushes past us on his way to the door.

"Thank you!" I call after him as he lets himself out.

He closes my door without a word.

"Wow, he's a real charmer, isn't he?" Miguel asks as he locks the door.

I choke back laughter. I can't remember ever laughing in this apartment before Miguel arrived.

* * *

Late Sunday afternoon, as we're both relaxing on the sofa, me with a book, Miguel on his laptop, there's a knock on my door. Miguel gets up to see who's there. "They're here," he says. He glances back at me before he starts on the deadbolts.

The door opens and in walks a stunningly beautiful

girl about my age, with long silky black hair pulled up in a high ponytail and beautiful dark eyes lined with kohl. She's dressed in distressed denim shorts, white sneakers, and a burgundy University of Chicago hoodie.

When she sees me, she removes a pair of wireless earbuds from her ears and tucks them into her hoodie's front pocket. "Hi." She smiles hesitantly. "You must be Ruby."

Standing, I nod. "Yes. Hi."

Right behind her is a man carrying a pair of dumbbells. He's dark haired too, with a trim beard. He's wearing jeans, boots, and a form-fitting black T-shirt. "Where do you want these?" he asks Miguel.

"Over there is fine," Miguel says, pointing to a corner of the living room, beside the TV.

The new guy sets a pair of the biggest dumbbells I've ever seen on the floor, then turns to me.

"This is Jason Miller," Miguel tells me. "And his girlfriend, Layla Alexander. Guys, this is Ruby Foster, my client."

"Nice to meet you, Ruby," Jason says. Then he looks to Miguel. "I'll be right back. I've got one more trip to make."

Miguel nods. "Thanks. Do you need help?"

Jason waves him off. "No, I could use the cardio." He chuckles, then kisses Layla on the cheek. "Be right back, babe."

She nods and watches him walk out the door.

"Would you like to sit down?" I ask Layla, motioning to the sofa.

Layla sits. "Thanks."

"Can I get you something to drink? Coffee, tea, or a soft drink?"

"Water would be great," she says. She sits with her hands clasped in her lap. She seems nervous.

"Still or sparkling?" I ask.

"Still," she says.

"I'll get it," Miguel says as he heads for the kitchen.

I sit again. A moment later, Miguel returns with a glass of chilled water for Layla.

"Thanks," she says before she takes a sip, then sets her glass down on a coaster on the coffee table.

Pumpkin appears out of nowhere and jumps up onto the coffee table, almost knocking her glass over. She grabs it up before there's a spill.

I scoop Pumpkin up and set him on my lap. "Sorry about that. This guy has no manners at all. You're not allergic to cats, are you? If he's bothering you, I can—"

"Oh, no, it's fine. He just startled me, that's all. I like cats." She reaches out to scratch Pumpkin behind his ears, and he leans into her touch, purring loudly.

Pumpkin takes the attention as an invitation and walks across my lap and over to hers.

Layla laughs when he rubs his head against her hand, begging for more scratches. "Aren't you a cutie?" she asks as she strokes Pumpkin's back. He arches his body, pressing closer to her.

"He likes you," I say.

Layla grins at me. "The feeling is mutual."

Jason returns with a plastic crate filled with two pairs of dumbbells, both smaller than the first set. He sets these weights down beside the others. "There you go," he says to Miguel. Then his gaze immediately goes to Layla. "Everything all right?" he asks her.

Layla laughs as Pumpkin brushes his head against her chin. "I think I made a new friend."

Jason smiles as he watches Layla interacting with Pumpkin.

"Can I get you something to drink?" Miguel asks his friend.

"Water would be great," Jason says. "Whatever Layla's having."

It's nearing dinner time, so I invite Jason and Layla to stay and eat with us. We end up ordering takeout from a local Turkish restaurant. While we wait for the food to be delivered, we play a few hands of Uno at the kitchen table.

Several times during the game, Layla seems to lose her focus, her attention drifting off. At one point, she's staring across the room, completely lost in thought. The room grows quiet as we wait for her to take her turn.

Eventually, Jason lays his hand on her shoulder. "Layla, sweetheart?"

She flinches as she turns to face him. "What?"

"It's your turn, babe," he says quietly.

Layla's gaze flashes to me across the table, and for a moment she looks disoriented, as if she forgot where she was. "I'm so sorry," she says, looking visibly embarrassed.

"It's okay," I tell her. I have the feeling I'm missing something here.

"Do you want your earbuds?" Jason asks her.

She looks unsure. "Do you mind?" she asks me.

"Of course not. Go ahead." Now I'm really confused.

Layla fishes her earbuds out of her hoodie pocket, pops them in her ears, and fiddles a moment with her phone. I get the feeling she's selecting a playlist to listen to. She glances at me. "Thanks. They help me concentrate."

"No problem." When I smile at her, she smiles back, seemingly relieved.

Despite her attention being split in multiple directions, Layla wins the first game hands down. Miguel wins the second game.

Just as we finish the second game, our food arrives, and we spread our feast out on the table. We ordered an assortment of kebabs, roasted vegetables, and rice. The food smells divine.

Miguel and I raid the kitchen for plates and silverware. I happen to glance over at the table to see Jason and Layla deep in quiet conversation. I watch as he reaches out and gently caresses her cheek. Nodding, she closes her eyes and leans into his touch. My chest tightens as I watch them expressing their obvious affection for each other.

Dinner is very enjoyable. Jason and Layla are fun, easy-going people. I notice Layla's attention drifting off several times during the meal, and each time, Jason gently guides her back to the conversation.

"I like your friends," I tell Miguel later that evening, after they've gone and we're hanging out in the living room. I'm sitting on the sofa with my book in my hands, watching Miguel pick up the smallest of the three pairs of dumbbells that Jason brought over. He curls his left arm, then lowers it. Then he does the same with his right arm.

"How much do those weigh?" I ask.

"These are just ten pounds each. They're good for warming up."

I whistle. "I doubt I could lift ten pounds with just one hand."

He laughs, and I watch his biceps bunch and flex as he raises and lowers the weights. He's changed into a black, sleeveless T-shirt that gives me an unrestricted view of his muscles.

After he does a number of reps, as he calls them, with the ten pound weights, he trades them in for a bigger set.

"How much do those weigh?" I ask.

"These are twenty pounds each, and the other pair are thirty pounds each."

While he goes through his reps, I get ready for bed and change into my nightgown. When I'm out of the bathroom, he goes in to get ready for bed.

"Let's hope we have a quiet night tonight," he says as he comes out of the bathroom. He's wearing a pair of gray sweatpants and nothing else. *Bare chest.*

I look away so I don't get caught ogling him.

"Hey, speaking of tonight," he says, "do you want me to sleep in your bed again?"

I feel my face heating as I nod. "If you don't mind."

"No, I don't mind."

While I turn off all the lights, Miguel checks the door locks and turns on the security system. It's nearly midnight when we finally head to bed.

I climb into bed on my side. He turns off the bedroom light and slips into bed on his side. "Sleep well," he says as he gets comfortable on his back. His low voice sends a shiver down my spine.

"Same to you," I say. After I pop melatonin into my mouth, I turn onto my side, facing away from him, and more importantly away from temptation. It's hard enough for me to fall asleep at the best of times, but when there's a man I find very attractive in bed with me, it seems like a Herculean feat.

I close my eyes and desperately start counting sheep again.

15

Miguel

At three o'clock in the morning, all hell breaks loose. We're awakened by the blaring sound of a car alarm going off in the parking lot outside Ruby's bedroom window. Ruby sits up. I sigh as I swing my feet to the floor.

I walk over to the window and peer outside. "Shit. That's my car."

A couple of angry shouts from our neighbors adds to the din.

Ruby follows me to the living room and watches as I slip on my sneakers and a T-shirt, strap on my chest holster, and grab my key fob.

"You're not going out there, are you?" she asks. "Can't you turn the alarm off remotely?"

"Yeah, but I need to check on my car. Don't worry, I won't be gone long. Come lock the door behind me."

Ruby follows me to the door and lets me out.

I race down the stairs and to the back door and step out into the chilly night air. Sure enough, my headlights are flashing, and my car siren is shrieking. Something in my gut tells me this isn't a random event. I just hope they didn't break my windows.

"Shut that damn thing off!" a man yells out a ground floor apartment window.

I wave at him. "Sorry! I'm on it." I turn off the alarm, give my car a once over, and relock it. I don't see any damage. I think someone just bumped it.

Now that my headlights are off, I realize how dark it is back here. I glance up and notice none of the streetlights are working. It looks like someone busted out the bulbs. *Oh, shit.* This isn't good.

A moment later, someone rams his shoulder into my abdomen and sends me crashing onto the pavement. I gasp, struggling to catch my breath, as the air's knocked out of me.

A chunky black boot comes at my face, and I throw up my arm to deflect the blow. Then there are two of them kicking me, aiming for my head. I roll to my belly and strain to get up onto my knees, using my arms to shield my head and face. One of them just misses kicking me in the mouth.

I finally succeed in getting to my feet. I swing for the one wearing sneakers and clip his jaw, sending him onto his ass. Then I turn to fend off a hit from the other guy, who attempts a roundhouse kick. I grab his boot and twist, sending him to the pavement as well.

When I turn back, Sneakers is long gone, leaving me with just one assailant. Boots is back up on his feet, ready for another go-around. He manages to land a punch high up on my cheek bone before I punch him square in the jaw. He staggers, catching himself on the hood of a car.

I can tell he's debating whether or not to take another run at me, but apparently he thinks better of it. He turns and runs farther into the darkened parking lot. I take a minute to catch my breath as my lungs billow for air. I feel the warmth of blood trickling down my cheek and my chin. *Damn it.* Ruby's not going to like this.

I'm starting to feel like someone doesn't want me here. But who?

My money's on Ruby's jealous neighbor. He's got the advantage of proximity, and I have no doubt that he's got a romantic interest in Ruby. I imagine he resents me moving in on his territory—literally.

I head back into the building and walk up the stairs. When I step back inside the apartment and Ruby gets a good look at my face, she gasps. "Oh, my God! Your face! What happened?"

I give her a wry smile. "I don't suppose you'd believe me if I said I tripped."

She frowns. "Hardly. Who did this to you?"

I shrug. "It was too dark to see their faces. I'd guess two hired thugs. They weren't even good fighters."

We're both surprised to hear a knock at this hour. I look through the peephole to see Rick standing outside Ruby's door, a scowl on his face. "It's Rick." He knocks again, loudly, so I unlock the door and open it. "Yes?"

Rick pushes his way into the apartment. "What the hell was that noise outside?" He glares at me. "What the hell happened to your face?" Without waiting for a response, he turns his attention to Ruby. "Why's this guy still here?"

Ruby swallows hard. "He's a friend."

"I'm just visiting," I say. I don't like the way he's talking to Ruby, like she's done something wrong.

"The lease specifically states that you can't have long-term visitors," Rick says.

"He's only been here a few days," she says.

Rick turns his attention back to me. "Look, I don't put up with bullshit in my building. No boyfriends moving in, no roommates who aren't on the lease. I don't know what you're up to, but whatever it is, you can just stop. I want you out of here by morning, you got that?"

Ruby eyes me warily, clearly intimidated by this guy.

"I'm not going anywhere," I say. "I'm Ruby's guest, and I'll stay as long as she wants me to. Do you have these rules written into the lease?"

I stare Rick down until he finally shakes his head.

"Then you can't kick me out of here."

"Fine. You want me to call the cops?" he asks. "I'll tell them you're disturbing the peace."

I shrug. "Go right ahead. We both know they're not going to do anything. I haven't broken any laws. By the way, both of the bulbs in the parking lot are out. You might want to get on that."

Rick jabs his index finger in my direction. "You better

watch yourself. If you cause any more commotion, I'm calling the cops."

"It wasn't Miguel's fault," Ruby says. "Someone tried to break into his car, and the alarm went off. He went outside to shut it down, that's all. Stop accusing him of things he didn't do."

"I'm not going to warn you again," Rick says to me. "Watch yourself." And then he storms out of the apartment, slamming the door behind him.

Ruby rushes forward to lock the door. "I'm so sorry about that."

"It's not your fault. He's an ass."

She laughs. "I'm not going to argue with you on that one." She surprises me when she takes my hand and pulls me to the bathroom. "Come on. Let me get you cleaned up."

I'm perfectly capable of cleaning myself up, but it's kinda nice having Ruby fuss over me like this.

Once we're in the bathroom, she flips on the light and maneuvers me to the sink. "Hold still," she says as she starts digging inside the linen closet and pulls out a washcloth, a tube of antibiotic ointment, and a little box of pink Band-Aids.

She turns on the tap, tests the water, and when it's

warm, she wets the washcloth and dabs at my cheek and lip. When I wince, she winces. "I'm so sorry, Miguel. I'm trying to be gentle."

"It's fine," I say, and that's when I realize my lower lip is starting to swell.

I bite back a laugh. I just got jumped by two guys, and Ruby's worrying about being gentle with me. After she cleans the blood off my face and smears some of the ointment on the cut on my cheek bone, she applies a pink bandage.

"There's blood on your T-shirt," she points out as she reaches for the hem and lifts it up. I take over, raising the shirt above my head and pulling it off. She takes it from me. "I'll wash this in the morning, see if I can get the blood out. I'll try, but no promises."

When she's done tending to my face, she surveys her workmanship. My bottom lip is throbbing like a bitch, and I can tell I'm going to have a black eye.

I think she catches us both by surprise when she reaches up and brushes my hair back from my forehead. "I'm so sorry," she says, as if it's her fault I got jumped.

It's not. I capture her hand in mine, stunned by how small and fragile it feels in my grasp. "You have nothing to be sorry for. It's not your fault."

"I can't help but think this has something to do with my stalker."

"Maybe. Maybe not. Still, it's not your fault. Zero."

She stands in front of me, gazing up into my eyes. There's a wealth of emotion swirling around in her beautiful blue eyes. This close to her, I see her eyes are flecked with hazel. I could get lost in those eyes. Hell, I want to. I'm aching to.

I clear my throat, hoping to break the spell before I do something stupid that we'll both end up regretting.

"We should get back to bed," she says. Her voice sounds odd, as if it's coming from far away.

"Yeah, good idea. Morning will be here before we know it." I follow her out of the bathroom, switching off the light on my way out.

She climbs into bed first, and I follow.

As usual, I'm lying on my back when she turns to me and raises up on her elbow. "Miguel?"

"Yes?"

She leans in close and presses her lips to my cheek. "Thank you. No one has ever done more for me than you have."

My heart crashes into my ribs, and I'm at a loss for words. How do I respond to that without sounding sappy? *This is nothing. I'd do anything for you. All you have to do is ask.*

I honestly don't know what to say, so I do what feels right in the moment. I slide a hand behind her neck and draw her closer. And then I lean forward to meet her halfway and kiss her.

She gasps softly, and then her eyelids drift shut. She leans into the moment, her lips clinging to mine. She tastes like peppermint, and my body responds like she's oxygen and I'm suffocating.

When I attempt to deepen the kiss, she pulls back, her eyes flashing wide open in surprise. She touches her lips. "Wow."

Wow? That's not the usual response I get when I kiss a woman. Then something dawns on me. "Ruby, have you ever had a boyfriend?"

When she shakes her head, I want to kick myself. Of course, she's never had a boyfriend. She hasn't left her apartment in two years. And before that, she attended both high school and university online from her home. When would she have had time to get out and mingle? *Meet someone? Never.*

She looks mortified. "I'm sorry. I shouldn't have—oh, my God, I'm sorry. Please forget this ever happened, okay?" And then she turns and lies on her side facing away from me.

Shit. "Ruby, I—"

"No, don't say anything. Please."

* * *

I can't sleep. Not only did I fuck up with Ruby, but I'm racking my brain trying to figure out who's stalking her—and why.

I could kick myself for misreading Ruby's intentions. She gave me a simple peck on the cheek, like she'd give to a friend. It wasn't an invitation of a sexual nature. And I misread the cue and kissed her. Really kissed her.

And the car alarm tonight? That was directed at me. Someone hired those two thugs to jump me. Probably the same person who hired that kid to throw rocks at Ruby's window. Right now the only suspect I have is Darren. He clearly thinks I'm encroaching on his territory. He's been pretty upfront about his feelings where I'm concerned. But I have zero proof.

I roll onto my side to face Ruby. I think she's finally asleep. Her breathing has been steady and even for the past hour. Damn it, I shouldn't have kissed her. It was so damn presumptuous of me. I've worked so hard to earn her trust, and I might have thrown all that away in one impetuous mistake. I'm surprised she didn't ask me to go back to sleeping on the couch.

I turn onto my back and start counting backward from one hundred. Maybe the sheer boredom of it will put me to sleep. *One hundred, ninety-nine, ninety-eight...*

The first thing I notice when I wake the next morning is a soft, warm weight pressed against my right side. I don't even need to open my eyes to know it's Ruby. I can smell her strawberry shampoo. I lie still, careful not to move, careful not to wake her. I want to enjoy this moment for as long as I can.

16

Ruby

When I wake up the next morning, I see that Miguel's side of the bed is empty. I lay my hand on the sheet where he slept and find it cold. The memory of him kissing me last night returns with a rush, and I'm both thrilled and mortified.

He kissed me!

My face heats up as a wave of dizziness washes through me. Surely he didn't mean to. Why would he? I'm a mess. A neurotic, agoraphobic, paranoid mess. I live like a hermit, shut away from the rest of the world. From *life*. The only time I see the light of day is when I look out my windows.

I climb out of bed and pull my robe on over my nightgown. Then I sneak across the hall to the bathroom to pee and brush my teeth. I hear sounds coming from the living room—Miguel huffing, breathing hard, grunting. He must be lifting weights. After brushing the tangles from my hair and putting it up in a pony tail, I leave the bathroom and head to the kitchen.

Sure enough, Miguel is lifting dumbbells, alternating arm curls, his biceps bunching and flexing.

"Good morning," he says breathlessly as I pass by.

I glance back at him, forcing a smile on my face. "Good morning." Then I get a glimpse of his face—at his black eye, the swollen cut on his cheek, and his swollen lower lip. He got hurt last night because of me, and I feel awful. "How's your face? Does it hurt much?"

"It's nothing," he says, brushing off my concern. He lowers both dumbbells to the floor, then straightens and puts his hands on his hips as he tries to catch his breath. He's dressed in a pair of black shorts and a sleeveless T-shirt which is all very distracting.

I continue to the kitchen where I put on a pot of coffee. "Would you like some coffee?"

He nods as he leans down to grab the dumbbells again. "Yes, please." Then he grimaces as he resumes lifting.

I wonder if he's sore from last night. I try not to stare as I go about making coffee—try and fail miserably. My gaze keeps going to his mouth, and I remember the feel of his lips on mine. I can't imagine anyone better to share my first kiss with.

While the coffeemaker is doing its thing, I go get dressed—jeans and a T-shirt. When I return from my bedroom, there's a knock at the door. I freeze. No one should be knocking at my door at this early hour.

Miguel sets his weights down and goes to look out the peephole. "It's Darren."

The hint of disgust in his tone makes me smile. Still, I'm surprised Darren is here. "He should be at work already." I nudge Miguel out of the way and open the door. Darren's dressed for work in a navy-blue suit, white dress shirt, and a blue-and-white striped tie. He looks flustered.

"Darren, what's wrong?"

He looks over my shoulder, and I can only assume that Miguel's standing behind me. "He's what's wrong," Darren says with a scowl. "What happened last night, Ruby?

What was all that commotion out in the parking lot?"

"Miguel's car alarm went off. When he went out to turn it off, he was jumped by two men."

Darren scowls at Miguel, then turns his attention back to me. "He needs to go," he says in a rushed whisper. "He's trouble, Ruby. He's not good for you. Just look at him. He's little more than a thug." He checks his watch. "I have to go to work. But trust me, Ruby, you need to get rid of him. Today. Just tell him to *leave*."

"*You* need to leave," Miguel says from behind me. His voice is deep and rough.

Darren narrows his eyes at Miguel, then looks at me one last time before he turns and heads for the stairwell.

I close the door and lock it.

"Don't you think he seems a bit fixated on you?" Miguel asks as he returns to his weights.

"You still consider Darren to be a suspect."

He nods. "I do. His interest in you seems a bit more than just neighborly. He's jealous."

I turn to face him. "Jealous? Are you serious?"

"I'm dead serious. I think he sees me as moving in on his territory."

"That's utterly ridiculous." I can't help smiling at the notion. I wouldn't mind being Miguel's territory. "First, there's absolutely nothing between me and Darren. We're simply neighbors. And second, *please*. As if you would be interested in someone like me." I laugh at the thought, but Miguel doesn't even crack a smile.

"Why wouldn't I be interested in someone like you?" He almost sounds offended. When he says this with a straight face, my heart starts racing.

He can't be serious. I nod toward the kitchen. "I'll start on breakfast."

Miguel lowers the weights. "I'll do it. You made breakfast yesterday."

"No, it's okay. I need something to do. You've already done so much for me."

Between that unexpected kiss last night, and Darren showing up this morning, my mind is frazzled.

"I'll just make scrambled eggs and toast," I say. "Something easy."

"All right. That sounds good."

I jump when I realize he's right behind me. I didn't even hear him approach.

"Ruby?"

"Hmm?" I glance out the kitchen window at the park.

"I'm sorry about last night. I shouldn't have kissed you."

"Please, don't mention it. It's fine. There's nothing to apologize for. Let's just forget it happened." I'm so embarrassed I can't even bring myself to look at him. "It was just as much my fault anyway. I kissed you first."

"On the cheek," he clarifies. "You were just being nice. I took it as an invitation. I was wrong."

"Please, Miguel. Can we not talk about this?"

He hesitates, then exhales a heavy breath. "Sure. Okay." He stands there a moment, as if he's going to say more. But then he changes the subject. "I'll take out the trash. The can's pretty full." He pulls the bag out of the trash can and ties it off. "I'll grab your mail, too, while I'm out."

I nod. "Thanks. Wait! I have several paintings packaged up and ready to mail. You can put them in the outgoing mail cubby. I'll go get them." I run off to my studio to collect the small packages ready to go.

After I hand the packages to Miguel, I follow him to the door so I can lock up after he's gone. I wait by the door for him to return, watching out the peephole. When I see him approaching, I unlock the door and open it.

He doesn't look happy. When I reach for my mail, he pulls it back out of reach.

"What is it?" I ask. Obviously, something's wrong.

"There was a note in your mailbox. Something printed off a computer."

I hold out my hand. "Let me see it."

Miguel hands me a sheet of paper folded in thirds. I open it up to see these lines:

GET RID OF HIM.
YOUR MINE.

"He spelled *you're* wrong," Miguel observes.

I smile. "Seriously? You're correcting my stalker's grammar?"

He shrugs. "I guess so."

"Now do you believe me about the notes?"

"Yes."

"I know what you're thinking," I say.

"What?" he asks.

"That Darren did it."

"He certainly could have. So could Rick. Honestly, anyone could have. There's something else," he says, as he hands me a business envelope. "Who is Craig T. Martin, Esq?"

I immediately relax. "Oh, that's fine. He's my attorney."

"The envelope says *estate planning*. Why is an estate

planning attorney writing to you?"

"Because he manages my trust fund."

"What trust fund?"

"My mom left all of her financial assets to me in a trust fund. I'll have access to the money when I turn twenty-five."

"And when is that?"

"In two months."

"How much is your trust fund worth?"

"Five hundred million dollars."

His eyes widen. "Holy shit! And you're just now telling me this?"

"I didn't think it was relevant."

"What about your dad?"

"What about him?"

"You said your mom left all of her financial assets to you. She didn't leave anything in her will for your dad?"

I shake my head. "No. They really weren't getting along at the time. And besides, my dad is wealthy in his own right. I guess she figured he didn't need anything from her."

Miguel looks pensive, and I can just see the wheels turning in his head as he tries to make sense of it.

"I'm sorry I didn't think to tell you. I just don't think

about it often. It's always there, in the back of my mind. I guess I take it for granted."

Miguel hands me the stack of mail and, with a groan, runs his fingers through his hair.

"What's wrong?" I ask.

"I think we have our motive, Ruby."

"Motive for what?"

"For terrorizing you."

"Because of my inheritance? I don't see how that helps anyone."

"Oh, sweetheart," he says. "This changes everything."

17

Miguel

Well, now we have our motive. Someone's terrorizing Ruby to get access to her trust fund. And who would want to do that? For starters, it would have to be someone who *knows* about her trust fund. Someone like the guy who's been collecting her mail. "Does Darren know about your trust fund?"

"No." Ruby shakes her head. "I've never told anyone."

"So, who knows about the money?"

"My dad, of course," she says. "And Edward. He's the trustee."

"No one else? Not any other friends or family members?"

She shakes her head. "I don't have any friends. Neither of my parents has any siblings, and my grandparents have passed, so there really isn't any other family. I suppose my dad might have told someone, maybe one of his friends or a colleague. It's not a secret."

I run my fingers through my hair and blow out a breath. *This is about the money.* I know it is. Someone's angling to get control of her inheritance. My bet is still on Darren. If he'd managed to get her to date him, and eventually marry him, he'd have access to her money. "Has Darren ever asked you out on a date?"

I can tell by the shocked look on her face that the answer is *yes*.

She shrugs. "A few times."

"And what did you tell him?"

"I said no."

My mind is racing through all of the implications. "Have any of the envelopes you received from your attorney ever arrived opened or damaged?"

She looks thoughtful. "One of them looked like it got

chewed up in the automatic sorter at the post office. The envelope was mangled and taped shut when I got it. But that happens sometimes."

"Or," I counter, "Darren opened it himself and made it look like it had been shredded at the post office. If he did, then he knows about your trust fund."

Ruby starts to object, then stops. "I suppose it's possible."

"I don't think it's a coincidence that you have a stalker *and* you're about to become a very wealthy woman." I grab my phone. "I need to call Shane."

"Hey, Miguel," Shane says as he takes my call. "How's everything going with Ruby?"

"There have been some significant developments." I tell him about the car alarm last night and the two guys who jumped me.

"Are you injured?"

"Just minor cuts, abrasions, and a black eye. I'm fine. Shane, did Edward McCall mention to you that Ruby is going to receive a trust fund when she turns twenty-five? That's in two months."

"A trust fund?" He sounds surprised. "No, he never mentioned it. How much money are we talking about?"

"A lot, Shane. Enough to motivate someone to take

desperate measures to try to gain control of her assets."

"How much are we talking about?"

"Five hundred million dollars."

Shane whistles. "Half a billion, with a *b*? I'm surprised Edward didn't mention that. This changes everything."

"I'd say we found the motive."

"I think you're probably right. So, who knows about the money?"

"Allen Foster knows, as well as Edward, as he's the trustee. Ruby says she hasn't told anyone. I have a strong suspicion that Ruby's neighbor, Darren Ingles, knows. He's been on my radar screen since I arrived. I think he resents my presence in Ruby's life. I wouldn't rule him out as a suspect."

"I'll have a talk with Edward and Allen. We need to know who else knows about the money, because there's our list of suspects."

"Agreed. People do crazy things when it comes to money."

"I'll do some digging into Allen Foster's finances. In the meanwhile, sit tight and keep doing what you're doing. Keep an eye out for more trouble as the stakes just increased significantly."

"Will do."

I end the call with Shane, then get on my laptop to do a little digging of my own, into Ruby's father and godfather.

* * *

That evening, after the dinner dishes are done and the kitchen's been cleaned up, Ruby and I decide to watch a movie—Black Panther. She drops down on the sofa, careful to leave a good two feet of open space between us. I think she's still self-conscious about the kiss we shared.

"Let's order coffee," she suggests, giving me a hopeful smile. "There's a coffee shop two blocks away that makes the best iced coffee concoctions ever. They're like dessert."

"You won't get any argument from me."

She's already on her phone placing an order. "What would you like?"

"Anything with caramel," I say. "Surprise me."

"Done." She smiles as she taps away on her phone. "Mocha peppermint with chocolate sprinkles and whipped cream for me."

As we start the movie, Pumpkin jumps up on the sofa

and curls into a ball between us, purring so loudly Ruby has to turn up the volume on the TV.

Thirty minutes later, there's a knock at the door.

"I'll get it," I say as I jump up from the sofa. When I glance out the peephole, I'm surprised to see Darren standing there holding our drinks. *Asshole.* I open the door and glance down the hall. "What are you doing with those? Where's the delivery driver?"

He shrugs. "I was just coming in from work when he arrived. I asked if they were for Ruby—I figured they were as she orders from them a lot. He said yes, so I offered to bring them up. It's no problem. I was coming this way anyway." He hands me the cups.

"Thanks," I say automatically.

Darren peers through the open door, undoubtedly looking for Ruby. When he spots her sitting on the sofa, he waves. "Hi, Ruby."

She waves back. "Hi, Darren."

"Goodbye, Darren," I say. Using my foot, I close the door in his face. *Asshole.*

"Here you go," I say, handing Ruby her cup. "Mocha Peppermint." The drinks aren't hard to tell apart because our names are written on the disposable cups in black permanent pen. Plus, hers has a mountain of melting whipped cream and sprinkles beneath the domed plastic lid. Mine doesn't. "Don't you think it's strange that Darren delivered our drinks to the apartment?"

"Not really," she says. "He's done it before. He's just trying to be helpful."

That's not how I see it. I think he's being presumptuous and territorial. Or maybe *I'm* the one being territorial. I glance at Ruby just in time to see her take a sip of her drink.

"Mm," she says. She pulls her straw out and licks the whipped cream off it.

Immediately, my dick hardens. Yeah, I've got it bad for her.

Ruby picks up the remote and resumes the movie while I sit down. I have to shift in my seat to relieve the pressure on a very inconvenient erection. My mind isn't on the movie, though. It's bugging the hell out of me that Darren delivered the coffees to us. The suspicious part of my brain is working overtime. *Or maybe it's the jealous part.* "Do you order coffee from this shop a lot?"

Ruby nods. "More than I should. They're my guilty pleasure." She takes another sip. Again she pulls her straw out of her cup to lick the whipped cream, getting some of it on her upper lip in the process.

Watching her lick her straw only heightens my arousal. I can't help imagining her tongue licking—*okay, just stop it. Pay attention to the movie.*

Ruby takes a long, leisurely sip before setting her cup on the coffee table. "How do you like yours?"

I try my iced caramel latte, and I'm pleasantly surprised. "It's good. Really good."

Pumpkin stands and jumps onto the coffee table, flicks his tail, and knocks Ruby's drink over in the process.

"Crap!" When I jump to my feet, Pumpkin bolts from the room, disappearing into Ruby's bedroom. I run to the kitchen to grab some paper towels. As I'm mopping up the puddle of coffee, which is running off the table onto the rug beneath, I notice Ruby is just sitting there, leaning back against the sofa cushions, staring in the direction of the TV screen. She doesn't seem the least bit fazed by her spilled drink puddling on the floor. "Ruby?"

I pat her knee. "Ruby?" When she doesn't respond, warning bells go off in my head. I switch on the lamp on the end table and look her in the eyes. "Ruby?" I shake her gently but get no reaction. My anxiety skyrockets as I grip her chin and make her look at me. "Talk to me, honey."

Ruby's head lolls back, and she stares up at me with

glassy eyes. "Miguel?" Her voice is slurred. She starts to reach out to me, but her hand falls limply to her lap. "Wha—" She starts shaking, and I notice sweat beading on her forehead.

Shit!

I grab my phone and call 911. While the call is connecting, I send a text message to Shane.

Me – Ruby's ill. Calling 911. Taking her to ER

Shane – I'll meet you there

When the 911 operator answers, I give her Ruby's address and all the information she asks for. "Caucasian female, 24 years old, approximately five-seven, one hundred thirty pounds. She's unresponsive, shaking, sweating." I eye her spilled coffee cup. "I think she's been drugged."

The operator asks me what she took.

"She didn't *take* anything, but she just drank some coffee from a local coffee shop, and I think it might have been spiked with something. As soon as she took a few sips, she zoned out on me."

I continue trying to get Ruby's attention, to get her to respond to me, but she's barely conscious. When she does try to say something, the syllables come out slurred and unintelligible.

"Stay on the phone with me, sir," the operator says. "I'm sending a squad to your location."

While we wait for the EMTs, I sit with Ruby, holding her in my arms as she continues to shake. She's mumbling, but I can't make out any of the words. I feel utterly helpless. The only thing I can do is hold her. "It's okay, honey. Help's on the way." I press my lips to the crown of her head. "Just hang in there. You're going to be all right." But even as I say that, I wonder who I'm trying to console—her or myself.

My stomach knots with fear.

Ten long, interminable minutes pass before there's a knock at our door. Carefully I release Ruby and jump up to let the EMTs in. Two of them, a man and a woman, rush into the apartment.

I stand back to give them room to work as they take her vitals and radio the information to the hospital. The female EMT calls on her radio for assistance with transporting the patient. A few minutes later, two firefighters appear at Ruby's door, carrying what looks like a wheelchair. The four of them place Ruby in the chair and securely strap her in from head to toe.

Seeing Ruby like that—so pale and lifeless—is unnerving. On impulse, I take the ruby ring off her finger and slip it into my pocket. She'd be heartbroken if that got lost.

I grab my phone, wallet, and keys. "I'm riding with you."

"Keep up," the woman says as the firefighters carry Ruby out the door.

After verifying that Pumpkin is still under Ruby's bed, I close the bedroom door to keep him safely contained. He's got water and a litter box in there to tide him over. After locking up the apartment, I follow the others down the stairs. There's an ambulance waiting out front, lights flashing, along with a firetruck and a police cruiser. A cop is directing traffic.

After the firefighters load Ruby into the ambulance and transfer her to a gurney, I'm instructed to climb into the front cab with the driver.

I text Shane to let him know we're en route to the hospital.

Shane – On my way. I'll notify Foster and McCall

When the ambulance pulls up to the entrance to the ER, Ruby is wheeled directly into the emergency treatment area. I try to stay with her, but I'm stopped at the front desk by a woman wanting Ruby's information. I give her as much as I can.

Shane arrives minutes later and joins me at the counter. "How is she?" he asks me.

"She was unresponsive when we arrived. I think she's had an overdose."

Shane scowls. "How in the hell is that possible?"

I recount everything that happened. "She didn't drink that much, Shane. Just a few sips. I can't imagine what would have happened if she'd consumed more."

Shane shakes his head. "But how?"

"I'll tell you how," I say, shock giving way to anger. "Ruby's neighbor, Darren, intercepted the drinks from the delivery person and brought them to her apartment. He could have spiked Ruby's coffee easily."

"But why would he drug her? That makes no sense. How is that going to help him in any way?"

"What the hell's going on?" Allen Foster bears down on us from the entrance to the ER, his expression furious.

"That's Ruby's father," I say to Shane.

Allen Foster grabs my shirt, his grip on my neckline practically choking me.

Shane gives me a curt shake of his head. *Don't respond.*

It kills me to stand there passively while Foster glares at me.

"Let him go, Mr. Foster," Shane says in a low voice.

Foster releases me and steps back to glare at Shane. "Who the hell are you?"

"I'm Shane McIntyre." Shane offers Foster his hand.

Allen Foster refuses to shake hands. Instead, he grits his teeth and turns his attention back to me. "What the hell happened to my daughter?"

"I'm pretty sure she was drugged," I say.

Foster's eyes narrow on me. "How?"

"We ordered coffee from a local shop. Shortly after she started drinking hers, she lost consciousness. I think her coffee was spiked with something."

A woman wearing light blue scrubs comes through the treatment doors and says, "For Ruby?"

"I'm Ruby's father," Allen says, pushing forward. "How's my daughter?"

"Would you come with me, please?"

Foster follows the woman into the treatment area.

I start pacing, running my fingers through my hair. "That son of a bitch."

Shane sighs. "Miguel, I know he's hard to deal with."

Feeling frantic, I keep pacing, dragging my fingers through my hair. "How in the hell could I have let this happen?" I feel sick.

Shane grabs my arm. "There's no way you could have

anticipated this. Don't blame yourself."

"Of course I blame myself! She's my responsibility, and I fucked up!" I lower my voice when I notice people are staring. "But why would Darren drug Ruby? What could he gain from hurting her? Or worse?" I point in the general direction of the treatment area. "She could die, Shane! We don't know how much of the drug she consumed." I blow out a breath.

"We need to know the stipulations of the trust fund," Shane says. "We need to find out what happens to the money if Ruby dies before her twenty-fifth birthday."

"Edward McCall would know. He's the trustee."

Shane claps his hand on my shoulder. "You stay here and wait for news. I'll contact Edward and see what I can find out."

I nod. "I'm not leaving until I know Ruby's okay."

A few minutes later, Foster returns from the treatment area.

"How is she?" I ask him.

He nails me with a grim look. "She's still unconscious. They said she's in serious, but stable condition. She's being treated for a drug overdose—*gamma* something. I forget what they called it."

"Gamma-hydroxybutyrate," I say. "GHB."

"Yeah, that. They found the drug in her blood, as well as alcohol. Apparently, alcohol magnifies the effects of the drug."

My chest tightens painfully. I'm almost afraid to ask. "Is she going to be okay?"

Foster shakes his head. "The doctor said it's too soon to tell. They'll know more when she regains consciousness."

"Can I see her?" I ask.

Allen Foster looks at me like I'm nuts. "See her? Hell no, you can't see her! I'll make sure you never see her again. You almost got her killed!"

Before I can respond, Shane joins us. He clearly heard Allen's last remark. "Mr. Foster, Miguel's quick action saved your daughter's life."

Foster turns his ire on Shane. "He was supposed to be protecting my daughter, and yet he *let* someone drug her!" To me, he says, "You stay the hell away from my daughter, do you hear me? If you go near her again, I'll call the police."

Foster storms off, leaving me speechless. I'm worried sick about Ruby, I have no idea how she's doing, and I doubt her father is going to keep me informed. And because of patient privacy laws, I can't even inquire. I turn to Shane. "Now what?"

"Be patient and try not to let Foster get under your skin." He lays a hand on my shoulder. "For now, since he's her next-of-kin, Allen's calling the shots."

I feel so helpless. "Her father's going to do everything he can to prevent me from seeing her."

"Don't worry," Shane says. "Ruby's an adult. Once she regains consciousness, she'll decide who she wants to see."

We grab seats in the waiting room and hope for news on Ruby's condition.

Not long after, a man in a dark suit, white shirt, and dark tie approaches, pulling something from his jacket pocket. He flashes a police badge. "Miguel Rodriguez?"

I nod. "That's me."

"I'm Detective Dale Cartwright, Chicago PD. I'd like to ask you a few questions about Ruby Foster."

"Sure." I glance at Shane, who's listening intently. "What would you like to know?" My pulse kicks up. This isn't good.

"What can you tell me about Ruby Foster's drug overdose?"

My body tenses as my heart pounds. "Ruby didn't overdose," I ground out. "Someone *drugged* her."

"You were there when it happened?" he asks.

"Yes."

The detective looks pensive. "We need to talk."

18

Ruby

I crack open my eyelids and find myself staring at an unfamiliar ceiling made of white tiles and recessed lights. My heart starts pounding. *Where am I? This isn't my apartment!*

Panic sets in, along with a crushing weight on my chest.

I can't breathe!

Frantically, I look around at white walls, unfamiliar furniture, machines beeping constantly. There are wires and tubes attached to my right arm. I'm lying on a bed, but it's not mine. The mattress is too firm, and the room smells strongly of disinfectant.

I'm outside.

I'm vulnerable.

It's unsafe.

One of the machines standing next to the bed starts beeping rapidly, the sound shrill and piercing.

A woman dressed in a white uniform rushes into the room. "Ruby, it's okay, honey." She reaches the foot of my bed and squeezes my foot. "You're in the hospital, but you're going to be fine." She comes around to the side of the bed and lays a gentle hand on my shoulder. "Try to relax, honey. Your pulse is through the roof. Just take a deep breath. You're okay."

The lights are so bright, I shut my eyes, but not before I catch a glimpse of a stranger standing beside the bed—an older African-American woman with short white hair. A nurse maybe? Off in the distance, I hear a female voice on the loudspeaker, calling for someone.

This is a hospital.

"Ruby, can you hear me?" The woman gently squeezes my shoulder. "Ruby? You're in the hospital. You're going to be all right."

My heart is pounding so hard my chest aches. I try to remember what happened, but my mind is too muddled. I remember bits and pieces—feeling dizzy, sluggish, like I was slogging through quicksand. I was watching a movie with Miguel and then everything went fuzzy. *Miguel!*

"Just try to relax, dear."

"Where's Miguel?" I ask, my voice cracking.

She pushes a button and says, "Ruby Foster's awake. Call Dr. Callejo. And someone find her father. Check the waiting room." The woman pats my arm once more. "It's okay, Ruby. Just relax. We'll find your father."

"No!" I shake my head. "Miguel! I need Miguel."

"I'm sorry, but I don't know who that is," the woman says. "Your doctor is on her way."

My eyes burn as they flood with tears. "I want to see Miguel."

"Ruby, are you all right?"

I turn to see my father standing at the foot of my bed. He looks… worried. "Dad, where's Miguel?"

"He's gone."

My stomach sinks. "What do you mean, he's gone?"

"He's gone, Ruby. Just like that, he left. He quit."

My heart aches. *Miguel can't leave me. Not like this. Not without saying goodbye.* "I need to see him."

"You don't need him. You're coming home with me where you'll be safe. It was a mistake to let you move out in the first place. You're not capable of taking care of yourself."

My lungs seize up on me and suddenly I can't get enough air. "I'm not moving back home."

"Yes, you are. End of discussion, Ruby."

A pretty brunette with short dark hair, dressed in a white lab coat, walks into my room. She smiles warmly. "Ruby! I'm so glad to see you're awake. I'm Dr. Callejo. I'll be taking care of you here in the ICU." She stops in front of the machines I'm connected to and frowns as she reads the printouts. "Your pulse and respiration rates are still pretty high. How are you feeling?"

"Fine. I want to go home. Please, I *need* to go home."

The doctor looks at my father, who shakes his head.

"Ruby," Dr. Callejo says, "I'll be happy to release you just as soon as we make sure you're all right. You had a close call, young lady. I want to make sure there aren't any lingering effects from your overdose."

"Overdose?"

"You overdosed on gamma hydroxybutyrate and alcohol. That's a dangerous combination. You're lucky you didn't consume more than you did."

"That's impossible. I don't take drugs, and I don't drink alcohol."

"Someone drugged you, Ruby," my father says. "I think I can guess who."

"Drugged me?" *Oh, my God, my coffee?*

"Mr. Foster," the doctor says. "Can I ask you to wait outside? I'd like to examine Ruby."

As soon as my father leaves, Dr. Callejo steps forward. "Ruby, can you tell me what month it is?"

My mind is muddled, and it takes me a moment to think. "It's June."

The doctor nods. "Good." Then she proceeds to check my eyes. "Follow my finger. That's right. Keep looking at my finger."

After the doctor leaves, the nurse—Doris, according to her name tag—asks me if I need anything.

"My phone," I tell her. "Do you know if anyone brought my phone?"

Doris opens the door to a cabinet and searches the contents of a large plastic bag. "I'm sorry, honey, but I don't see anything here other than your clothes."

My stomach sinks. Without my phone, I have no way to contact Miguel.

After she sets a glass of water on the bedside table,

Doris dims the lights in the room. "Drink some water and try to rest. I'll check on you in a little bit." She pats my leg as she walks around the foot of the bed. "Everything's going to be okay. You'll see."

I'm desperate to talk to Miguel. Surely, he didn't quit. How could he just walk away from me without a word?

19

Miguel

Detective Cartwright sits in the chair beside me. "Ruby's father has filed a complaint with the police department accusing you of giving his daughter a dangerous mix of drugs and alcohol." The man pulls a small black notepad and a pen from his jacket pocket. "Why don't we start at the beginning? Tell me what happened tonight."

I tell him everything, from the moment the coffees showed up until we arrived here at the hospital.

He makes notes, saying nothing until I finish.

"So, you're claiming that Ruby's drink was spiked before it arrived at your apartment?"

"Yes." Then I give him the basic rundown, starting with when I was assigned to Ruby's case. "And you suspect her neighbor?" The detective consults his notes. "Darren Ingles?"

I nod. "He had both opportunity and motive."

"I see. Well, how about we start with Ruby's apartment?" He stands, gesturing for me to join him. "I'd like to see the crime scene. I'd also like to search her apartment."

"Go," Shane says. "I'll be here. I'll let you know as soon as I hear anything about Ruby's condition."

I rise. "Fine. Let's get this over with."

* * *

Detective Cartwright follows me to Ruby's apartment building. We both park in the rear lot and walk in together through the rear entrance.

"Her apartment's on the second floor," I say, motioning toward the stairs. "Do you mind if I check her mailbox first?"

Cartwright nods. "Go right ahead."

He follows me down the center hallway to the mail room at the front of the building. I glance inside her mailbox and find a single sheet of white paper folded in thirds. I gesture to the note. "This is how her stalker sends her messages."

Cartwright grabs a pair of latex gloves out of his jacket pocket and pulls them on. He reaches in, grabs the sheet of paper, and reads it. He shows it to me.

I WARNED YOU

"Warned her about what?" Cartwright asks.

"Getting rid of me. The last message she received said 'Get rid of him.' Meaning me."

The detective studies her mailbox. "These boxes aren't adequately secured. Anyone could slip something in them." He glances toward the stairs. "Let's go see the apartment."

We head upstairs to Ruby's apartment. I let us in and disarm the security system. Cartwright heads right for the coffee table and starts taking pictures. There's spilled coffee on the table, along with the tipped over cup. The spill has dried for the most part, a large milky brown stain spreading across half of the surface of the table.

"Ruby's cat knocked over her cup, spilling most of the contents. He probably saved her life. She didn't take more than a few sips before she was overcome."

I start to reach for the toppled cup, but Cartwright stops me with an outstretched arm. "Don't touch it."

With gloved hands, he lifts the cup to peer inside. Thanks to the plastic domed lid, there's still some liquid remaining in the cup. "Hopefully it's enough to analyze," he says as he pulls an evidence bag from his jacket and slips the cup in. "And we can get some fingerprints off this as well."

"My prints are on her cup," I warn him. "Darren's too, as he brought the cups to our door. Plus the prints of the delivery person and whomever handled her cup at the coffee shop."

Cartwright nods. "I'll need to get a statement from the neighbor. If we have his corroboration that he brought the cups to this apartment, there's reason to add him to the list of potential suspects."

I like this guy. He seems to be following the facts and not jumping to conclusions, in spite of whatever Foster might have said to him, accusing me. Cartwright seems open-minded, and he's giving me the benefit of the doubt.

"Do you mind if I search the apartment?" he asks.

I nod. "Go right ahead. Neither one of us has anything to hide."

"Then have a seat," he says, indicating the sofa. "Don't get up, and don't touch anything."

I do as he says, hoping to get this over with as quickly as possible. I want to get back to the hospital to find out more about Ruby's condition.

Cartwright starts in the kitchen, methodically searching every drawer and cupboard. He's still wearing gloves, and the whole situation is surreal. I feel like I'm in a cop show.

He proceeds to search the rest of the apartment, starting with the living room, then on to Ruby's bedroom, the bathroom and linen cupboard, and the art studio.

Finally, he returns to the living room and pulls off his gloves. "Nothing."

"I told you." I motion in the direction of Darren's unit. "The apartment you should be searching is right next door."

"Well, let's go pay your neighbor a visit."

We proceed next door, and Cartwright knocks, but there's no answer.

"Looks like no one's home," the detective says. "I'll apply for a search warrant."

"Am I free to go? I need to get back to the hospital to check on Ruby."

Cartwright nods. "Yeah, go ahead." He narrows his eyes. "I don't think I need to say it, but—don't leave town, okay."

"Yeah, I assumed as much. Don't worry. I'm not going anywhere."

As soon as Cartwright leaves, I return to Ruby's apartment to check on Pumpkin. He's still under Ruby's bed. "Hey, buddy," I say as I reach under the bed to scratch his chin. "You okay?"

He stares at me for a long moment, blinks, and starts purring.

"How about a snack before I take off?"

Pumpkin follows me to the kitchen, and I put a bit of food in his bowl and give him fresh water. "I'll be back to check on you," I tell him.

Before I leave, I grab Ruby's phone and charger and stuff them into a bag. I know she's going to want her phone. After locking up the apartment, I head for the stairs, hoping to run into Darren, but no such luck. I wouldn't be surprised if he's gone into hiding.

As I'm getting into my car, my phone chimes with an incoming message from Shane.

Shane – She's in stable condition. They're monitoring her vitals.

I hightail it to the hospital and walk into the ICU waiting room, where I find Shane. "Any word?" I ask as I sit beside him.

He shakes his head. "Nothing more since I texted you. Foster isn't being very forthcoming."

A little while later, Allen Foster walks into the waiting room and heads for the coffee machine.

I follow him. "How's Ruby?"

Allen turns to glare at me. "None of your business. Why haven't the police arrested you yet?"

"Maybe because I didn't do it. Answer me—how is she?"

He ignores me as he waits for the machine to fill his cup.

I'm tempted to grab him and shake the hell out of him, but I know that won't get me anywhere except perhaps in a jail cell.

"Allen!" Edward McCall races into the waiting room, out of breath and flushed. "How is she? Is she okay?"

Foster's eyes narrow on Edward, then he turns them

on me. "Both of you, get out of here. You have no business being here."

"How can you say that, Allen?" Edward says. His expression falls, and he looks genuinely hurt. "You know how much Ruby means to me. She's like family."

"Well, she's not your family!" Allen practically spits out the words. "She's *my* daughter. And I say you're not welcome here." Then Allen looks my way. "Both of you, just leave."

Allen takes his cup of coffee and stalks out of the waiting room, heading back toward the intensive care unit. I start to follow him, but Edward grabs my arm.

"Don't waste your time, son," Edward says. He pats my back.

"I need to know she's okay." My stomach knots.

Edward shakes his head. "Don't worry. She's going to be okay." He squeezes my shoulder. "You just have to have faith."

Edward gets some coffee and takes a seat by a window.

I return to sit with Shane. "It's my fault she's hurt. I was supposed to protect her, and I let her down. She put her trust in me, and I let someone hurt her on my watch."

He shakes his head. "You couldn't have anticipated

this." Shane pats my back. "We need to plan for what happens after she's released from the hospital. She can't go back to her apartment. It's not safe."

"I could take her to my apartment. Our building is secure." Shane owns the building I live in. Quite a number of McIntyre Security employees live there, including many of my friends.

"Better yet," Shane says, "how about I lend you two the use of a three-bedroom apartment in my building, free of charge? You'll have plenty of space, and she'll have room to paint."

"Thanks. That sounds perfect. I'll talk to Ruby about it. She's going to be upset that she was taken from her apartment. I don't know how she'll take to the idea of moving to another apartment."

A middle-aged African-American woman dressed in a nurse's uniform walks into the waiting room and addresses me. "Are you Miguel Rodriguez?"

I shoot to my feet. "Yes. How's Ruby?"

"She's doing well. She's asking for you. She's about to be moved to a private room. Her doctor wants her to stay just overnight for observation."

"Can I see her?"

"As soon as she's moved, I'll let you know the room

number."

The nurse leaves, and I blow out a heavy breath. Finally, some news. Now that she's awake, Foster won't be able to prevent me from seeing her. I resume pacing, too antsy to sit still.

It's almost an hour later before the nurse returns to hand me a slip of paper with Ruby's new room number.

"She's eager to see you," she says, winking at me. "I can see why." She smiles before turning away.

Shane stands. "When you see her, talk to her about moving to my building. Once she agrees, let me know, and I'll arrange for her belongings to be moved to the new apartment. I'll make sure it's ready by the time she's released."

"I can't thank you enough, Shane."

"You don't need to thank me." He lays a hand on my shoulder. "I had a feeling you were the right man for the job."

By the time I get to Ruby's new room, I find Allen Foster standing outside her door, talking on his phone. When he spots me coming, he ends his call and pockets his phone. "What are you doing here?" he asks.

"What do you think I'm doing? I'm here to see Ruby." I gesture to her door.

Foster shakes his head. "You're wasting your time. Ruby doesn't want to see you."

I've reached the end of my patience with this guy. I don't care that he's Ruby's father. "Let her tell me to my face."

As I start toward her door, Foster moves in front of me, physically blocking me. His face tightens into a grimace. "I'm not telling you again." He practically growls the words. "If you don't leave right now, I'm calling security and having you forcibly removed."

"I'd like to see you try. I'm not leaving until I see Ruby."

"Miguel!" Ruby's muffled cry comes from inside the room. "Miguel, is that you?"

"I'm here, Ruby! I'm coming." I glare at Foster. "Let me pass."

20

Miguel

Suddenly, Ruby's door opens, and a nurse steps out. The young blonde woman singles me out. "Are you Miguel?" she asks, holding the door open.

I nod. "I am."

"Ruby's been asking for you. You can go on in."

I walk past Foster and enter Ruby's hospital room. At first I don't see her because the privacy curtain is drawn around the bed. I sweep past it, and there she is, sitting up in bed, leaning on a stack of pillows propped against the headboard. She smiles the instant she sees me.

I walk over to her and, unable to help myself, I cup her face in my hands and look her over. She's paler than usual, and there are faint shadows under her eyes, but otherwise she looks good. She looks amazing. "Ruby." I need a second to rein in my emotions. "Are you okay?"

She nods. "I'm fine. I'm tired, but otherwise I'm okay." She reaches up and covers my hands with hers, gripping them hard. Not pushing them away. Not pushing *me* away. Her gaze searches mine almost frantically.

There are so many things I want to say.

I'm sorry I let you down.

I'll never let it happen again.

But none of those words come out. Instead, I lose myself in her beautiful blue eyes. Time stands still. My heart slams into my ribs, and my chest constricts as I realize how close I came to losing her.

She's not even mine, but I realize right then, in that moment and with absolute clarity, that I want her to be mine.

"Miguel." Her voice is a breathy sigh, and she tightens her grip on my hands, as if she's afraid I'll release her.

She's not pushing me away.

I lean forward and kiss her forehead. "Ruby."

And still, she's not pushing me away. In fact, her hands slide off mine and she reaches for me.

I pull back and stare into her eyes, which are glittering now with unshed tears. "I was so scared," I admit.

"Please don't quit," she says, her voice shaky. "Don't leave me. I can't do this without you."

"*Quit?* I'd never quit on you. Your father told me you didn't want to see me."

She shakes her head adamantly. "I never said that! He lied to you."

Fury surges inside me. "He played us against each other." My fingers slip into her hair. "I've been fighting to see you since you arrived at the hospital. Your father wouldn't let them tell me anything about your condition, and he barred anyone else from seeing you. He wouldn't even let Edward see you."

She leans forward and rests her forehead on my shoulder. "Please take me home." Her body shudders. "I can't be here, Miguel. It's not safe." Suddenly, she stiffens. "Pumpkin!"

I kiss the top of her head. "Don't worry, honey. The cat's fine. I made sure of it."

She smiles gratefully. "You did?"

"Of course I did." I lean forward and kiss her lightly.

"I'm already making plans to take you somewhere safe as soon as you're released."

"Where? What are you talking about?"

"Your apartment building isn't secure, sweetheart. It's not safe. At least not until we know who tried to poison you."

"But I have to go back to my apartment. It's the only place—"

I cup her face. "Ruby, do you trust me?"

Her eyes lock onto mine. "Yes," she says without hesitation.

"Then trust that I have somewhere safe to take you."

"Where?"

"Shane has offered us the use of a three-bedroom apartment in his building in the Gold Coast. That's my building, too."

She shakes her head. "The Gold Coast? I can't afford that."

"It's free of charge, as long as we need it. This is a well-secured building. Layla and Jason live there, plus many more of my friends. You'll be safe there."

Her eyes widen again, filled with apprehension. "What about my things? What about Pumpkin? And my art supplies? I need to work."

"I'll have all of your belongings moved to the new apartment. It'll feel just like home, I promise. It'll be just like what you have now, only more space and a lot more secure."

She's shaking now, so I sit on the side of the bed and pull her into my arms. "You'll be safe there," I whisper against her forehead. "I promise."

"You'll be with me?"

"Of course. I'm not leaving you."

She nods. "Okay."

"Before I forget—" I reach into my pocket and pull out her ring. "—I've been keeping this safe for you." I slip her mother's ring onto her finger.

The hospital room door opens and Allen strides in. When he throws the privacy curtain wide open, Ruby flinches. I realize she's using the curtain as a barrier between herself and the rest of the world. It's her shield right now, her safety net. The only one she has.

Foster doesn't even spare me a glance. "Ruby, this is getting ridiculous. You're coming home with me. Your apartment is hardly safe, is it?" Foster glares at me. "You could have died, no thanks to this idiot."

"It wasn't Miguel's fault!" Ruby tightens her hold on my hand. "He saved my life. If he hadn't called 911 when he did, I probably wouldn't be alive right now."

"That's so convenient, don't you think?" Foster asks. He nods to me. "Miguel gets to play the big hero and ingratiate himself with you in the process. Who do you think drugged your coffee in the first place, Ruby?" He stares at her expectantly, as if he assumes she'll agree with him.

Ruby looks away, gazing out the large picture window. "I don't know, but it wasn't Miguel."

"You are so damn gullible," Foster says. "He's already under investigation by the Chicago PD. He's their number one suspect."

Ruby looks at me in shock. "Is that true? Are they investigating you?"

"I've been questioned by a detective, yes. But I'm not a suspect."

She brushes her thumb over the back of my hand. "That's ridiculous," she says to her father. "Miguel had nothing to do with it."

Foster crosses his arms over his chest. "Tell that to Detective Cartwright."

I've heard enough. Foster's just going to continue aggravating Ruby, and she's going to continue defending me, and the two of them will keep running circles around each other.

"That's enough," I say to Foster. "You need to leave. You're upsetting Ruby." He scowls at the both of us before he turns and stalks out the door.

Ruby covers her face with her hands. "Miguel, I'm so sorry."

"It's okay." I put my arm around her and draw her close. When she melts into me, I smile. "Everything's going to be fine."

"Were you really interviewed by the police?"

"Yeah, but it was fine. I met with one of the detectives at your apartment. He searched the place, with my permission. I hope you don't mind. I knew he wouldn't find anything incriminating because there's nothing to find. He's working on getting a warrant so he can search Darren's apartment."

"You still think Darren's behind this?"

"I do."

Ruby shakes her head in disbelief. "I can't believe he'd do this. It doesn't make any sense. Why in the world would he want to hurt me?"

"I don't know, but I'm going to find out. In the meanwhile, we need to make plans to move you to the new apartment."

She squeezes my hand. "My doctor said I might be able to go home later today."

"I'll let Shane know. He's going to get your belongings packed and moved to the new apartment before you're released."

She doesn't look happy about the idea of moving.

"You trust me, right?" I ask.

She nods.

"Then trust me when I say this is the right thing to do."

"Okay."

She smiles, and I find myself mesmerized once more, unable to look away. Her eyes search mine, and I feel a surge of electricity sparking between us. This has got to be my imagination. There's no way she's feeling a tenth of what I'm feeling. Unable to help myself, I reach out with my free hand and brush her silky hair back from her face. When her eyes drift closed on a sigh and she leans into my touch, my chest tightens. I suddenly feel hot, flushed, and my pulse starts racing.

I pull my hand back. "It's late, and you need to sleep."

"You're not leaving, are you?"

"No." I gesture to the sofa. "I'm going to park myself right there all night long. I'll be here in the morning when you wake up. Now get some sleep, *cariño*." I reach over to switch off the lights before I lean down to kiss her forehead.. "Goodnight, Ruby. Sleep well."

* * *

At eight A.M., I slip out of Ruby's room to call Shane to get the wheels in motion. I also get his okay to ask Charlotte Mercer to come sit with Ruby while I go supervise the move. Charlotte—Charlie—is a good friend of mine, and she lives in my building. I figure it's a good idea to introduce her to Ruby.

When I call Charlie, she jumps at the chance. "Anything to get me off this boring surveillance job I'm doing," she says with a laugh. "I'll call Jake to get a replacement."

I slip back into Ruby's room just as she's waking. "Good morning, *cariño*. How'd you sleep?"

"Not bad."

When I tell her all about Charlie coming to spend the day with her, she looks apprehensive.

"But she's a stranger," she says.

"I know, but I trust her with my life." I reach out for Ruby's hand and give it a gentle squeeze. "You'll like her, I promise."

I help Ruby walk to the bathroom, where she takes a shower and puts on her hospital gown. When she comes out, her breakfast has arrived. She sits up in bed to eat an omelet, toast, and some fresh fruit, and she sips a cup of coffee.

About an hour later, there's a knock on Ruby's door. I get up from the sofa to answer the door. "Hey, Charlie. Come on in."

Charlie follows me into the room and peers around the privacy curtain. She smiles at Ruby. "Hello, Ms. Foster. I'm Charlotte, your company for the day. My friends call me Charlie."

Charlie is in her early thirties. She was born and raised in Atlanta, and despite having moved away when she graduated high school and joined the Army, she still has a hint of a southern accent and the manners to boot. Everyone likes Charlie. She has a beautiful smile that puts everyone at ease right off the bat.

She's dressed casually in jeans and a pink T-shirt. Her curly black hair is up in a bun, with a few corkscrew curls hanging down. She's about Ruby's height, but that's where the physical similarities end. While Ruby's fair and blue-eyed, Charlie's skin is a warm brown and her big eyes are dark pools of obsidian.

"Call me Ruby, please," Ruby says. "It's a pleasure to meet you." Her gaze flickers over to me.

I give Charlie a rundown on the players at hand—namely, Allen Foster and Edward McCall. Those are the only ones who might visit Ruby while I'm gone. "Call me if there are any issues," I tell her. "And don't let Ruby's father—Allen—browbeat you. He's a bit of a jerk."

Charlie nods. "Got it. Not a problem. Ruby and I will do just fine."

I give Ruby a light kiss. "I almost forgot!" I reach into the bag I brought from the apartment and retrieve her phone and charger, handing them to her. "I thought you'd want these. Call me if you need me. I'll be back just as soon as I can."

She gazes up at me and nods. "Thank you! I feel naked without my phone."

Once I'm sure Ruby is handling this okay, I leave her in Charlie's very capable hands.

As I'm heading for the parking garage, I spot a familiar face at the end of the hallway near the door to the stairwell. Not just one familiar face, but two—Allen Foster and Darren Ingles, in a heated argument.

What the hell?

What are the two of them arguing about? And more

importantly, how do they even know each other?

I change direction before either one of them spots me and hitch a ride downstairs in an elevator.

It looks like Darren and I need to have another talk.

21

Ruby

Everything's better now that I've been reunited with Miguel. I'm still fuming because my dad lied to me about Miguel quitting. But I guess it's not a surprise. My father and I haven't seen eye to eye in a long time. I assume it's because he blames me for my mother's death because that's when his demeanor toward me changed.

Before we lost Mom, my dad and I were pretty close. We had a good and loving relationship. Why else would he change toward me? Even as a child, I could recognize his disdain for me. I've tried to broach the subject with him over the years, but he refuses to discuss it. He says it's all in my head—that everything between us is fine. But I know he's lying.

Charlie seems nice. She takes a seat on the sofa. "Miguel told me you're an artist."

"Yes. I paint miniature custom portraits, mostly people's pets and kids. What about you? What do you like to do?"

"I'm a bit of a tech nerd," she says. "I play a lot of video games and watch movies."

While we're chatting, my phone chimes with an incoming text message.

Miguel – Movers have arrived. They're packing your stuff now.

"Good news, I hope?" Charlie asks.

"It's from Miguel. He says the movers have arrived and are packing up my things."

"I hear you're moving into my building. You're going to love it. It's convenient to shopping and restaurants, and the building has all the amenities you could want, including a state-of-the-art fitness center and a pool. And, it's only a couple of blocks from Lake Michigan.

You'll love the view."

I smile, trying to look enthusiastic. Charlie obviously doesn't know I don't go outside.

"You guys will probably be just down the hall from my apartment."

"It'll be nice to know someone in the building. Miguel says the security is tight. Is that right?"

"It is. There are cameras all over the public places on the property. To enter the building, you have to pass through a security gate in the main lobby where IDs are checked. Visitors have to be approved. A lot of my friends live in that building. I think you've met Jason and Layla already? They live there. We get together often at each other's apartments to hang out, watch movies, cook out, or just chill. You're welcome to join us."

Charlie pauses, looking at me thoughtfully. I wonder if my apprehension is showing.

"Of course you don't have to," she says. "No pressure. You do you."

"Miguel has a lot of friends, doesn't he?"

She nods. "He's very popular. When we go out, girls practically throw themselves at him."

I reach for my water glass, but it's almost empty.

"Here, let me get you some more," Charlie says. She

grabs the pitcher on the side table and pours ice water into my glass.

Even though I got a decent amount of sleep last night, I'm still tired. "Do you mind if I doze off a while?"

"Of course not," Charlie says. "Take a nap. Don't mind me." She gets up and turns down the lights before returning to the sofa. She holds up her phone. "I'll just read for a while."

I lean back on my pillow and close my eyes. I'm almost asleep when there's a quiet knock at the door. Immediately, I jump.

Charlie stands. "I'll get it." She disappears to the other side of the privacy curtain and speaks quietly to someone at the door. Soon she peeks around the curtain. "Edward McCall is here. He wants to know if you feel up to a visitor."

"Yes, definitely." Edward's someone I'm always happy to see.

Edward walks around the curtain holding onto a helium *get well* balloon. "Hey, kiddo." He smiles. "How are you feeling?"

"Much better. Just tired. I hope to be released later today."

"I brought you a little something to cheer you up." He

ties the balloon to the foot of my bedframe. "Are you sure it's safe to go back to your apartment? Would you like to come stay with me? You're always welcome, you know."

"Miguel has arranged for us to move into an apartment in his building." I give him the building's location in the Gold Coast.

"That's a fantastic piece of real estate, and it's very secure."

Charlie, who's back on the sofa reading, nods. "Absolutely."

"This is Charlie," I say, motioning to my babysitter. "She works for the same company Miguel does. She's hanging out with me until Miguel gets back from supervising the move."

Edward nods in approval. "Nice to meet you, Charlie." He pulls up another visitor chair and sits on the other side of my bed. He reaches for my hand and gives it a squeeze. "Is there anything I can do for you? Anything I can get you?"

"I don't think so. I'm just anxious to be released and return to some sort of normalcy."

"My apartment building isn't far from where you'll be staying," Edward says. "If it's okay, I'd like to come and visit you, see how you're settling in."

"I'd like that. Edward?"

"Yes?"

"Dad told me Miguel had quit. He lied to me."

"Your father does seem a bit stressed lately. More than usual, anyway. It's probably because he's worried about you. We're all worried about you. This attempt to drug you is concerning for us all."

I lower my voice. "What did I ever do to make him hate me so much?"

"Oh, honey, Allen doesn't hate you. You're his daughter—you're all he has left after Helen—" He breaks off here as shadows darken his blue eyes. He looks away. "Allen took her death hard. We all did. She was the glue that held us all together. Just be patient with him, Ruby. I'm sure he'll ease up once your stalker is caught."

22

Miguel

Shane performed a miracle getting a professional moving company to move Ruby's entire apartment full of belongings today on such short notice. I guess money talks. I imagine these people are being paid far more than overtime. They're here now at Ruby's apartment in Wicker Park, over a dozen uniformed people packing up her belongings.

Everything is going to the new apartment—every pot, every pan, everything in the bathroom, her bedroom, all the furniture and her clothes, every hanging plant, as well as the plants on the balcony. Even her wind chime.

Packing up her art studio is going to be the biggest challenge. Not only are her walls covered in small paintings, but the bookcase shelves are jam packed with supplies, everything from jars of paintbrushes, tubes of paint, blank canvases, art books, and numerous tools I can't even identify. They have four people working in her studio, taking reference photos so they'll be able to put it all back together in the new place. These people are professionals, working quickly and efficiently to sort, tag, and wrap everything securely before boxing it up, labeling it, and getting it all into the moving truck parked outside the building.

Jason and Layla come over at my request to collect Pumpkin and all his necessities—his food, cat bed, bowls, toys, and litter boxes. They'll keep him for us until the move is completed.

Jason observes the bustling activity in the apartment. "Shane must have called in some favors to get this arranged so quickly."

After my friends have collected all of the cat's necessities, I secure Pumpkin in his carrier. He meows in protest. "Sorry, pal. But don't worry. You'll be reunited with

Ruby before you know it."

Jason takes the carrier from me, lifts it, and peers inside. "Hey, little fella. Ready to go for a ride?"

Layla sticks her finger into the carrier, and Pumpkin rubs his face against it, purring loudly.

"Hey, he still likes you," I tell her.

She smiles. "Of course he does." She winks at me. "He has good taste."

Jason leans over to kiss Layla's cheek. "So do I."

The plan is for them to take Pumpkin back to their place, where they'll keep him until all of Ruby's belongings have been moved into our new apartment.

Our apartment.

I like the sound of that, but of course I have to remind myself this is only temporary until we're sure the ones responsible for drugging Ruby have been apprehended and she's safe. I imagine she'll want to return to her own apartment after this is all over.

"Call us when you're ready for him," Jason says. "We'll bring him to you."

As I let them out of the apartment, I walk down the hall to Darren's apartment and knock. There's no response. I knock again, loud enough to wake the dead. "Open the door, Darren!"

There's no response, but I guess that's not surprising. He's probably at work. I need to talk to him. I need to know what the connection is between him and Ruby's father. The sick feeling in my gut tells me it's not a good one.

I call Detective Cartwright and tell him I spotted Darren and Allen Foster arguing at the hospital. To my knowledge, the two men didn't even know each other, so I find it more than a little suspicious.

"I should have a warrant to search Ingles's apartment sometime today," Cartwright says. "As soon as we locate him, I'm bringing him in for questioning."

I return to Ruby's apartment to oversee the packing. The movers are doing a great job. Already they're starting to load stuff into the truck. Most of the materials in her art studio have already been packed.

The kitchen has been emptied. Her table and chairs are in the truck. The hanging plants are gone, packed up and ready for transport. The photos on the walls have been packed. It looks like the sofa, chair, and all the floor rugs are next.

Miraculously, they have everything loaded into the moving truck a little after noon. I follow the moving truck across town to the Gold Coast and direct them to park in the underground garage so they can use the oversized freight elevator to move everything up to our apartment.

While the movers are unloading the first of Ruby's belongings into the service elevator, I head up to the security desk in the main lobby to get the keys so I can run up ahead of the movers and unlock the apartment.

We have one of the bigger floor plans in the building—one with three bedrooms and a home office. I do a quick walk-through to make sure everything is clean and in order. The apartment looks freshly scrubbed. The floors are immaculate. The bathroom is clean, as is the kitchen and laundry room. Everything looks presentable. My hope is that when Ruby sees all her familiar belongings here, she'll feel at home.

The balcony off the living room faces east, and we have an unobstructed view of Lake Michigan.

Before long, the movers begin transferring everything into the apartment. They file into the place, one after another, each pushing a dolly filled with either furniture or boxes.

I call down to the front desk to ask someone from maintenance to come up and place hooks in the ceilings of the living room and kitchen so that her plants can be hung near the windows and balcony doors. One of the nice things about living in an upscale building like this is that services are available around the clock. All we have to do is make a call.

If the clothes washer stops working at midnight? No problem.

Got a clogged toilet at 3 A.M.? No problem.

Need plants hung at 1 P.M.? No problem.

I tell the movers where everything goes. While they're moving Ruby's things in, I ask Jason to help me move my bedroom furniture and work-out equipment to this apartment. Everything else—the living room furniture, TV, kitchen supplies, table and chairs—is Ruby's. I want her to feel safe here. I want her to feel like this is her *home*.

Our home, at least for a little while.

Finally, everything has been unpacked and put in its right place by 4 P.M. After the movers leave, I run down the hall to Jason and Layla's apartment to get Pumpkin. They help me bring the cat and all his accessories back to the apartment. I set him up in Ruby's bedroom, hoping that he'll be comforted being around familiar furnishings.

When I open the cat carrier in Ruby's new bedroom,

Pumpkin darts out of the box and immediately runs under the bed. While Layla is setting up the cat box with fresh litter, I crouch down beside the bed to peer at Pumpkin.

"Hey, little guy. This is your new home—at least for the time being. Nothing's changed. All your stuff is here. Ruby should be here soon. I'm sure she'll give you lots of love and attention to make up for the upheaval you've experienced."

I leave the cat with bowls of fresh water and food. Before I leave, I grab a change of clothes and a pair of shoes for Ruby and stuff them into a duffle bag. She's going to need something besides a hospital gown to wear home.

By the time I get to the hospital, the staff are passing out patients' dinners.

When I walk into Ruby's room, I'm glad to see her sitting up and eating. "Did you miss me?" I toss the duffle bag on the bed.

Ruby's eyes widen in surprise. "Miguel!" She shoves the bedding aside and jumps out of bed in nothing but her hospital gown and bare feet. She runs to me and throws her arms around me, hugging me tight.

I wrap my arms around her, hugging her back just as tightly. "I take it you did."

She looks up at me with teary eyes. "You have no idea. How'd it go?"

"Everything went just as planned. We've been moved into the new apartment, and all of your stuff is in place. I think you'll like it. Pumpkin is anxiously awaiting your return."

I glance across the room at Charlie. "Everything go okay while I was gone?"

Charlie nods. "Fine. Ruby's friend Edward stopped by to see her, and her nurses checked on her a couple of times, but other than that, it's been just the two of us." She stands and tucks her phone in her back pocket. "I'll take off now so you two can catch up."

Charlie gives Ruby a hug before she heads out. I walk her to the door. "No one else came to visit? Not Ruby's father, or someone named Darren?"

She shakes her head. "No one. Just Edward, and he seemed nice enough. Ruby was glad to see him."

"Good." I give Charlie a hug. "Thanks for coming. I had a feeling you and Ruby would hit it off."

"Anytime, pal." She play punches my arm. "Just holler if you guys need me for anything after you get settled into your new place. You know I'm just down the hall."

After Charlie's gone, I close Ruby's door and return to

her bedside. She's back in bed now, her gown covered by the bedding. I take a seat on her bed.

Ruby reaches for my hand and squeezes it. "Thank you, for everything. Especially for taking care of Pumpkin."

I brush the backs of her fingers with my thumb. "You don't need to thank me. I'm happy I can help. I just want you to feel safe and happy."

23

Ruby

After I finish eating dinner, I change into the clothes that Miguel brought me. Now I'm just waiting for my doctor to give me my discharge instructions and sign my release papers. I hope it won't be too much longer.

My mind is dwelling on the fact that I'm not going back to *my* apartment. I'm going to Miguel's apartment building. All my stuff is there, so that should help, but it's the actual trip to the apartment that has me most worried—leaving the hospital and driving across town to the new building.

Other than my recent ambulance ride, I haven't been in a vehicle in two years. I was unconscious during the trip to the ER, so I didn't know what was happening. But now, I'll be fully aware of what's happening. I'm not sure how I'll handle being outside and in a car. At least I'll be with Miguel.

I'm in the bathroom finishing up brushing my teeth and hair when I hear voices coming from the other side of the bathroom door. Especially one particular voice, heated and loud.

I open the bathroom door and step outside. "Dad? What are you doing here?"

My dad is standing at the foot of the bed, glaring at Miguel, who's sitting on the sofa. As he turns to me, his expression softens. "Sweetheart, I came to ask you nicely to come home with me where you belong."

I shake my head and look to Miguel, then back at my dad. "I'm sorry, Dad, but no."

"I'm your father, Ruby. You belong with me, not with this—" he gestures to Miguel— "opportunistic—"

"Stop it, Dad. Miguel's my friend. You have no right to talk to him like that."

Miguel steps between us. "Mr. Foster, Ruby has made her wishes clear. She's not going home with you, and you certainly can't force her. She's an adult. She can make her own choices."

My father's expression turns glacial. "Do you want me to have you declared mentally incompetent? Is that it? Because I will."

I suck in a sharp breath, shocked that he'd say such a thing to me. Yes, I have issues, but I'm not mentally incompetent.

"All right, that's enough," Miguel says, advancing on my dad. He points to the door. "It's time for you to leave, Mr. Foster. If you can't be civil, then you can go."

I have to admit, Miguel can be rather intimidating when he wants to. He hasn't even raised his voice, and yet my dad takes a step back, not quite so confident now.

After my father storms out, I collapse onto the bed. "I can't believe he said that."

Miguel sits beside me and takes one of my hands in his. "Try not to let him get to you. He's bluffing."

The daytime nurse, Rita, pushes a wheelchair into my room. "I've come to go over your discharge instructions with you and give you your release papers. You're free to go."

Miguel asks Rita if she'll stay with me while he goes out to the parking lot to bring his vehicle up to the front doors. Then he'll come inside and escort me out to the car.

It's not long before Miguel returns.

"Have a seat," Miguel says to me, gesturing to the wheelchair.

I try not to laugh. "Do I really have to?"

He nods. "Sorry, but it's hospital policy. I have to wheel you out to the car."

I take a seat, feeling very self-conscious. Miguel hands me his duffle bag. "Hold this for me?"

"Sure." I set it on my lap and rest my arms on it.

Miguel squeezes my shoulder. "Just relax, honey. I'll have you home in no time." He rolls me toward the door. "Just focus on Pumpkin and how happy he'll be to see you again." When we reach the privacy curtain, he reaches out to grasp the fabric. "I'm going to open the curtain now, okay?"

I nod and close my eyes. I hear the whirring sound as the curtain slides open. The chair moves. I can tell we're in the hallway because the air feels a bit cooler, and now I hear the chatter of distant voices, conversations in other rooms, down the hallway, probably in the waiting room.

"Doing okay?" he asks.

"Mm-hmm." My eyes are still closed, and the longer we're out here—out in public—the more my stomach hollows out, and I feel sick. My ears start to ring.

I hear the ding of an elevator, then the whoosh of the doors. I can tell he's wheeled me inside. There are other people in here with us, murmuring quietly about where they're going to go for dinner.

As the elevator descends, Miguel rests both hands on my shoulders, squeezing gently. It's only then that I realize I'm shaking and breathing heavily.

"It's okay," he murmurs quietly. "Try to relax."

Still, I keep my eyes closed and go to my happy place—my apartment. Only it's not my apartment we're going to. It's a different place filled with my things. I focus on my art supplies, performing a mental inventory of all my brushes and paints and palette tools. I catalog my favorite paintings that hang in my studio. I think about the commissions I'm working on—customer orders that are behind schedule now because of my hospitalization.

The elevator doors open, and the wheelchair moves forward. Ambient noises are louder now. I hear voices all around me. I smell flowers—roses, to be exact. I smell coffee. We must be passing through the hospital lobby.

"We're almost at the door," Miguel says in a low voice. "Once we're outside, I'll wheel you to the front passenger door of my car. I'll help you into the vehicle, and we'll be off. Okay?"

I nod. What other choice do I have? *None.*

Miguel brushes his hand gently over my hair. "You're doing great. Just a little farther. Hang in there."

When Miguel wheels me out through the doors, I'm hit with a gentle breeze and the scents of the outdoors. I smell fresh-cut grass and flowers, car exhaust. The heat from the sun warms my face.

I'm outside for the first time in two years.

The shaking intensifies.

When I hear the screech of tires, followed by someone leaning on their horn, I flinch.

Miguel rubs my back. "It's okay. Just some idiot behind a wheel."

The wheelchair glides to a gentle stop, and then I hear the beep of his vehicle doors unlocking. At the sound of the car door opening, I shudder, as it brings back memories of the carjacking.

"In you go," he says. He takes the duffle bag off my lap and tosses it into the rear seat of the vehicle. He takes my hand, helps me stand, and guides me into the front passenger seat.

I still haven't opened my eyes. If I can't see it, it's not real. I'm not really outside.

I'm shaking when he secures my seat belt. He lays his hand on my thigh. "Ready to go?"

When he reaches for my hand and brings it to his mouth to kiss the back of it, a shiver courses down my spine.

"You're trying to distract me," I say, fighting a smile.

He chuckles. "Is it working?"

I laugh. "Maybe a little."

"I'm going to shut your door, then walk around to the driver's side and get in. Then we'll be off. We'll be home before you know it."

My door closes. A moment later, the driver's door opens. The vehicle rocks slightly as he slides into the driver's seat. As soon as the engine starts, we move forward, eventually surging into traffic.

"Don't you want to see where we're going?" he asks.

"No." I keep my eyes closed and focus on breathing. I think of Pumpkin, imagine his purring and the soft, warm weight of his body pressed against mine. I think of my paints, the colors, imagining how they mix together creating beautiful hues and shades. I think of my plants.

Oh, my God. My plants. "Did the plants get moved, too?"

Miguel pats my thigh. "Yes. Everything was moved over. You'll feel right at home, I promise."

The rest of the trip passes in a whirlwind. We drive down into a cool, dark space into what I suspect is an underground parking garage. My shaking intensifies, and I feel like I'm going to throw up. My mother was killed in a parking garage—they're dark, dank caverns filled with innumerable hiding places. Filled with monsters, like the one who took my mother from me.

The vehicle comes to a stop. Miguel turns off the engine, and then he comes around to my door, opens it, and helps me out.

He pulls me close and wraps his arms around me. "We're here. We'll take the elevator up to our floor, walk down the hallway, then enter our apartment. Okay?"

"Okay."

Our apartment.

I like the sound of that. I know he didn't mean it *that* way. This is just a temporary place—temporary for me and for him. Once my stalker is caught, I'm sure I'll go back to my own apartment, and life will return to the way it was before.

Miguel holds my hand. "Here's the elevator," he says.

"Step inside."

He steers me into the opening, and we turn to face the doors, which swoosh shut. The elevator car jolts, and then it begins to ascend swiftly and smoothly.

Eventually, we come to a gliding stop. The doors open, and Miguel leads me out. We turn left and walk down a carpeted hallway. A keyring jingles, then a door opens, and Miguel guides me inside. My eyes are still closed—have been since before we left the hospital.

"We're here," he says.

It's cool inside and smells like lemon-scented cleaner.

The door closes behind us, and I hear him turn the deadbolt.

Just one deadbolt.

"I'll ask maintenance to install more deadbolts," he says, sounding casual and very matter-of-fact. "And a chain lock."

My chest tightens as I nod. *He knows me. He gets me.*

"You can open your eyes now," he says quietly, his lips near my ear. His breath ruffles my hair, making me shiver. "You're safely home."

My heart is pounding as I prepare to see this place... this apartment that is filled with my things but isn't my apartment.

I open my eyes and glance around the living room, the kitchen, and the balcony.

And then I burst into tears.

24

Miguel

I wasn't sure what to expect when we arrived at the new apartment, but I certainly didn't expect this. The sound of Ruby's sobbing is breaking my heart. I really thought this would work. I thought having her things here would make her feel safe and comforted.

I pull her into my arms and hold her close. She presses her face against my chest, her hot tears soaking my T-shirt. "What is it?" I ask, feeling a bit lost.

I tried so hard to recreate her apartment in this place.

I tried to make it as familiar for her as I could to ease the transition. Obviously, I failed. I pull back, cupping her face, and make her look at me. "Please talk to me. What's wrong?"

Ruby turns and looks at her surroundings… the sofa, the chair, the coffee table, the floor rugs. Her TV hangs on the wall. Her plants hang from hooks in front of the glass balcony doors, and out on the balcony are her potted trees and containers filled with flowers and ferns. Her kitchen table and chairs are visible from where we're standing. The framed photo of Ruby and her mom hangs on the wall. Everything's here.

She wipes her cheeks with shaking hands, then gazes up at me. "It's—" She throws her arms around my neck and hugs me. "It's perfect, Miguel."

Relieved that I didn't mess this up after all, I slip my arms around her waist and hold her close. She's practically vibrating with emotion. "I wanted you to feel safe. I wanted you to feel at home."

I stare down into her beautiful blue eyes—red-rimmed now and tear-filled—and my breath stalls. My heart races, and I can feel my pulse thrumming through my body. She's looking at me like I just hung the sun and the moon for her. I brush tears off her freckled cheeks.

My fingers slide into her hair. And still, she keeps looking at me, expectantly, almost as if—

She reaches up and touches my face, her fingertip gentle as she traces my brow, then the edge of my cheek. And then she gently traces the curve of my lips. "Miguel."

There's so much emotion in the tone of her voice. *God, please tell me I'm not imagining this.*

I realize we're both frozen, both of us afraid to make a wrong move. I guess there's only one way to know. "Ruby?"

"Mmm?"

"Would you be terribly upset if I kissed you right now?"

Her lips curve into a smile, dimples appearing in her soft, freckled cheeks. "Not at all. In fact, I'd be more upset if you didn't."

Cupping her face, I lean down to press my lips to hers. Her mouth is trembling, her breath shaky, and yet she's clutching my arms. I test the water by deepening the kiss, and her hold on me turns into a death grip.

She's definitely not pushing me away.

Her lips part, taking the kiss to a whole new level, and my doubts and concerns about what's right and wrong go straight out the window. She wants this, just as much as I do.

When we hear Pumpkin's plaintive wail coming from one of the bedrooms, we break apart.

"Oh, my God, Pumpkin!" she says.

I take Ruby's hand. "Come on. Let's free Pumpkin and finish the tour."

As soon as we open Ruby's bedroom door, Pumpkin comes racing out. He practically throws himself against her legs, purring like a motorboat.

"You poor baby," she coos, scooping him up in her arms. "You must be terrified."

Ruby walks into her new bedroom and turns in a circle, observing every little detail. She opens her dresser drawers and the nightstand drawers. Everything is right where she left it. She opens the closet doors to find her clothes hanging just as they were at her place. Her shoes are lined up on the closet floor. Her shoeboxes filled with mementos are sitting on the overhead shelf. Even the curtains hanging in front of her window are from the other apartment.

I show her the middle bedroom, which is now her art studio. Everything's in place. All her canvases are hanging on the walls. Her worktable looks just like it did before. Her supplies are arranged on the bookcase shelves exactly as she had them.

She shakes her head. "I can't believe this. It's so perfect." She turns to me. "You did this. You told them to make it perfect."

I nod. "I wanted this place to feel familiar to you."

After she examines the linen closet and the bathroom, she stops in front of the door of the last bedroom, which is currently closed. "Is this your bedroom?"

I nod as I turn the knob and open the door. Inside the room is my king size bed covered in a gray comforter, two nightstands, lamps, and a dresser. She opens the closet door to see all of my clothes and shoes, everything from my closet is here. Even my gun safe has been moved here, stowed in the closet.

She eyes my bed and frowns. "I'm sure you're thrilled to have your own bed to sleep in again. No more sleeping on the sofa."

"It wasn't that bad." Actually, no. I'm not thrilled. Suddenly, having my own bedroom doesn't seem like such a great idea after all. I much preferred sharing a bed with Ruby, even if it was purely platonic.

Pumpkin springs out of Ruby's arms, jumps to the floor and starts rubbing against her ankles, purring loudly.

"I think someone wants his dinner," I say.

She nods and heads for the kitchen. Pumpkin follows her, darting between her feet in his exuberance. In the kitchen, she locates the cat food in the pantry and dishes it into his bowl. She tops off his water bowl and sets it on the floor next to his food.

Pumpkin devours his food, purring loudly in the process.

"How does he do that without choking?" I ask. "Speaking of food, are you hungry?"

"No," Ruby says. "I had enough to eat at the hospital. What about you?"

"I grabbed something after the movers finished. But I do think we should celebrate you getting out of the hospital and us moving into this apartment."

"What did you have in mind?"

I open the fridge and peer inside. "There's not much to choose from." I grab two bottles of sparkling water and hand her one. "I guess this will have to do. How about we sit out on the balcony and drink a toast?"

She looks apprehensive for a moment, but then she nods. "I hear the views from this building are amazing."

We carry our drinks outside and sit on the two chairs on the balcony.

"To us," Ruby says, holding her bottle up to me.

I tap my bottle to hers, and we drink.

While we sit quietly and enjoy the view, Ruby stares at the lake. "My parents used to take me to the beach when I was a kid. I loved the water." She smiles sadly. "That was a long time ago, when I still had my mom and before my dad hated me."

"Ruby, he doesn't hate you."

"Then how do you explain the way he treats me? The way he talks to me?"

That I don't have an answer for. She's right—it doesn't make sense. I reach over to caress the back of her neck. "No one could ever hate you."

She smiles at me. "You're just being nice."

"Have you been back to the lake since your mom passed?"

She shakes her head. "Dad and I never really did anything together after Mom died. Edward took me to the beach a few times, but eventually I stopped going anywhere. It was just too hard."

"You did well leaving the hospital today. I wasn't sure how that was going to go. You surprised me. I'm proud of you."

She smiles as she sips her sparkling water. "My eyes

were closed the entire time. That's hardly an act of bravery. It was more like an ostrich sticking her head in the sand."

She watches the sailboats and yachts on the lake, the people frolicking on the beach, the pedestrians and cyclists cruising along the paved path that borders the beach.

"Maybe we could walk down to the lake sometime," I say casually. "It's only a few blocks." It's just a suggestion. I'm not sure how she'll take the idea.

She doesn't respond, just keeps watching the activity on the lake. "I can smell the water, even from here. It brings back some good memories."

After we finish our drinks, Ruby waters all her plants, the ones hanging inside as well as the ones out on the balcony. When she comes back inside, she says, "I can't believe you managed all this in one day. Everything's perfect."

"Well, I can't take credit for that. The movers did all the work. Actually, the credit goes to Shane. He made it all happen."

She sets the watering can down just inside the balcony door before she turns to me and wraps her arms around my waist. "I couldn't do any of this without you."

I hug her back, but I don't say what I want to say. She may not be ready to hear it.

There isn't anything I wouldn't do for you.

Instead, I say, "You don't have to thank me. I'm happy to help." *How lame.* Those words feel so inadequate.

I stroke her hair, unable to resist the temptation. "Ruby, I—" I want to talk about our kiss earlier, but I stop myself. No matter how I look at it, I'd be taking advantage of her if I encouraged anything romantic between us. I'm all she has right now. I'm her lifeline. Her security, literally. It would be *wrong* of me to make things personal. Unprofessional. Inappropriate.

She lays her head on my chest, her ear right over my heart. I'm sure she can feel how it's thundering.

Unprofessional, I remind myself.

Inappropriate.

Abruptly, I change the subject, hoping to get us on more solid ground. "There are some things I need to do this evening." I need to talk to Darren Ingles. I have a feeling he's the key to figuring out who's trying to hurt Ruby. "Would you be okay if I asked Layla or Charlie to come stay with you while I'm gone?"

Ruby pulls back and gazes up at me. "What kind of things?"

I find myself staring into her eyes, unable to look away. "Investigative things."

She frowns. "You're referring to the person who drugged me."

"Yes. We need to find out who did it. You could have died, Ruby. Whoever did it needs to be held accountable."

"I'll be fine by myself. I don't want to trouble your friends."

I'm not comfortable leaving her here alone yet. "I'd feel better if someone was here with you. Just until you settle in, okay?"

"I don't need a babysitter. Besides, I'm really behind on my commissions, and I need to bury myself in my work and try to get caught up. You go do what you need to do. Don't worry about me. I'll be fine. Besides, I've got Pumpkin for company."

I sigh, recognizing defeat when I see it. If she's asking for some independence, I don't want to take that away from her. "All right. I'll text you Layla's number. If you need anything at all, you can call her. Her apartment is just down the hall."

Ruby lays her hands on my chest. "I'll be fine. You go."

25

Miguel

By the time I make it to Ruby's old apartment building, it's eight o'clock in the evening. I park behind the building and look for Darren's car, but it's not here. He's still not home.

I go inside and stop in the mailroom to pick up Ruby's mail. She's got a few pieces of junk mail and a water bill. I make a mental note to have Ruby's mail forwarded to the new address.

I run upstairs and knock on Darren's door, but there's

no response. I'm not surprised. So I sit outside his apartment door to wait for him to return. Unless he's skipped town—I wouldn't put it past him—he's bound to return home sooner or later. I just hope it's sooner. I don't like leaving Ruby alone right now.

Finally, half an hour later, I hear someone coming up the stairs. A minute later, I spot Darren. He looks awful. His face is flushed, and his suit is rumpled. He looks stressed out. He stops in his tracks when he spots me and his shoulders slump. "What do you want?"

I stand. "To talk to you."

"Where's Ruby?" He glances down the hall at her apartment. "Is she home?"

"She's not here, if that's what you're asking."

He doesn't bother to hide his surprise. "Why not? She's been released from the hospital. Where else would she be?"

"How do you know she was released?" Undoubtedly, he got the information from Allen.

Darren flinches, as if he just realized what he gave away. "I don't know for sure. I just assumed, since you're here—"

"Did Allen Foster tell you?"

Darren's eyes widen. "Who? Oh, you mean Ruby's father. No." Darren frowns. "Why would he tell me anything? I don't even know the man."

Liar.

"What were you doing at the hospital earlier, arguing with him? How the hell do you know Ruby's father?"

Darren pales. "I don't know what you're talking about."

I fist his tie and shove him against his apartment door. "I saw you at the hospital arguing with Foster. What I want to know is what you were arguing about."

He shakes his head. "I have no idea—"

I tighten my grip on his tie, putting pressure on his windpipe and cutting off his air. "What were you arguing about?"

He tries to pry my hand off him, but he's about as effective as a fly swatting a human.

"How do you know Allen Foster?"

Darren's face is turning red. "From work," he gasps. When I loosen my grip, he sucks in a breath. "We work for the same investment firm. He's my boss."

What the hell? "How long have you worked for him?"

Darren shrugs offhandedly. "I don't know. Ten years maybe."

Ten years. "And you just happen to be Ruby's neighbor?" That's too much of a coincidence to be believable.

"When did you move into this building?"

"About a year ago."

"So, after Ruby did. How in the hell did you end up living next door to your boss's daughter? Did Foster put you up to this? Did he tell you to move into her building?"

Darren nods.

"Why? To spy on her?"

"To keep an eye on her, yeah. Allen was worried about her."

An apartment door down the hall opens and closes, and a young couple I don't know walks toward the stairs. They wave and say hi.

"Open your door," I tell Darren after they pass. We don't need an audience. "You and I are going to have a little talk."

With shaking fingers, Darren fishes his keyring out of his trouser pocket and unlocks his door. I push the door open and shove Darren inside.

While he turns on a lamp, I shut the door behind me. "Sit!" I say, pointing to his kitchen table.

I don't know what the connection is between Darren and Allen, but there are a lot of dots that need to be connected.

Darren sits, looking ashen. He clasps his hands on the

table in front of him. He's perspiring like he's just run a marathon.

Foster and Darren are somehow connected.

Darren works for Foster.

Darren delivered the coffees to Ruby's apartment.

"You put the GHB and the alcohol in Ruby's coffee, didn't you? After you took it from the delivery guy, you spiked her drink."

Darren looks out through his balcony doors at the setting sun. "I didn't know what it was," he says in a quiet voice. "I swear I didn't know it would put her in the hospital!"

"Did Allen tell you to spike her coffee?"

Darren winces but says nothing. To my surprise, I realize he's struggling to hold back tears.

I reach across the small table and grab his tie. "Did he?"

He nods frantically. "Yes, it was Allen. He gave me a vial of clear liquid a little while ago and told me to put it in her coffee the first chance I got. When I saw the delivery guy from the coffee shop arrive, I took the cups from him back to my apartment, poured the liquid from the vial into hers, then delivered them to her apartment." Darren looks up at me, clearly stricken. "I didn't know what was in the vial. I would never do anything to hurt Ruby, I swear it!"

He seems genuinely devastated.

Darren starts crying in earnest.

I take the chair opposite his and soften my voice. "The amount of GHB you put in her drink was more than enough to kill her. It's a fluke that she's still alive, Darren. Let that sink in. You nearly *killed* Ruby. If she'd drunk more, she likely would have died. You're an accomplice to attempted murder. You realize that, right?"

Darren's gaze flashes up at me, his eyes wide with shock. "What—no! It was just supposed to scare her, that's all. That's all it ever was—he wanted her scared so that she'd move back home."

"Who, Allen?"

"Yes." Darren looks sick. "It was just supposed to scare her, that's all. I swear!"

"Why would Allen want to kill his own daughter?"

"She's not his daughter!" His words reverberate like gunshots in the quiet apartment.

"What are you talking about?" I sound as shocked as I feel.

Darren shakes his head. "She's not his child—not biologically, anyway."

"How?"

"After his wife died, Allen arranged for a paternity test. He'd always suspected Ruby wasn't his. After Helen died, he wanted to find out for sure. The test came back negative."

"Why did he suspect Ruby wasn't his?"

"Allen and Helen had a falling out at one point, and Helen moved out. They were separated for a couple of months, but they ended up getting back together. Helen was already pregnant then. She told Allen the baby was his—that she hadn't been with anyone else. Allen told me he didn't believe her, but he desperately wanted her back, so he kept his mouth shut. Then, after Helen died, he wanted to know for sure."

"If Allen Foster's not Ruby's biological father, who is?"

"Allen told me it was Edward McCall."

"Edward?" My mind is reeling with the implications. Helen Foster and Edward McCall? "Are you sure?"

"Allen seems to think so. He thinks they hooked up while he and Helen were separated."

"Does Edward know?"

"No. As far as I know, he has no idea. Neither does Ruby. Allen's the only one who knows. Well, besides me." Darren lays his hands flat on the table and looks me in the eye. "Please, you have to believe I'd never knowingly hurt Ruby. I—"

"Wait, why would Foster want Ruby dead?"

"He didn't, at least not in the beginning. But he wanted to gain control of her trust fund. The initial plan was for me to seduce Ruby and marry her. When that didn't seem to be working, Allen decided to scare her into moving back home with him."

"So, you're the stalker? You put the roadkill outside her door? You left the threatening messages in her mailbox?"

Darren nods. "But none of that seemed to be working, and Allen was running out of time. Ruby's birthday is in two months. Once she turns twenty-five, the trust fund money will be hers. He needs control of that money, desperately, before it's too late."

I feel almost numb as the pieces start to fall into place. "Why?"

"Allen's been stealing from his clients' investment accounts for years, and he needs to replace the funds before anyone finds out. But Allen's broke, and he can't pay the money back. If he gets caught, he'll spend the rest of his life in prison."

"And he's willing to kill Ruby to get her money?"

"I guess so—he's desperate. But I never signed up for

anything like this. I thought we were just scaring her. Allen's her only known next of kin," Darren says. "If she died without a will, her trust fund would automatically go to him."

"How does Edward McCall come into this?"

"He doesn't know anything. As far as he knows, he's just her godfather."

I let out a long sigh. "So, you were the one terrorizing Ruby all along."

Darren nods. "Partly me. Allen hired some kids to help. I was supposed to be her knight in shining armor. Her protector. And then you showed up."

I shake my head in disgust. "When I told Ruby you were at the top of my suspect list, she defended you. She said you were a good guy, that it couldn't be you. She thought I was nuts for suspecting you." I pick up my phone. "I'm calling Detective Cartwright of Chicago PD. You're going to tell him everything you told me."

Darren shakes his head. "No way. I can't. I'll lose my job. I'll lose everything."

"It's too late. You've already lost everything." I show him my phone screen.

He grows pale. "You're recording this?"

"Yep. Every word."

"I'm not going to be Allen's fall guy."

"It's a little late for that, don't you think?"

26

Ruby

After Miguel leaves to do his sleuthing, I stand at the balcony doors for the longest time and stare at Lake Michigan. I haven't been this close to the lake in years. As the sun crosses the evening sky, I watch how the light reflects off the water's surface. I envy the people playing on the beach, the kids splashing in the surf, the adults swimming out toward the buoys. I keep thinking back to what Miguel said about us walking down to the beach.

I'd love nothing more.

But I can't do it. It's too much to even contemplate.

But I do know this—if there was anyone who made me feel safe enough to try, it would be Miguel.

I head to my art studio and take a good look around. Everything's right where it should be. I marvel at the movers' attention to detail. As I take my seat at the worktable, Pumpkin curls up in the little cat bed at my feet. All my supplies are within reach, and I pick up right where I left off on my newest commission—an older gray tabby cat with a white patch on his chest.

I've been working for about an hour when my phone rings. I check the screen, then immediately accept the call. "Miguel, hi!"

"Hi, Ruby." He sighs. "I just wanted to let you know I'm going to be tied up for a while this evening. Can I have Layla come hang out with you until I get home?"

"It's okay. I'm fine. Honestly. I'm working on a painting, and Pumpkin is keeping me company. The movers did a phenomenal job with my art supplies."

"Good. I'm glad."

"Is everything all right?" There's something odd about his voice. He sounds uncharacteristically subdued.

"Everything's fine. I'm making progress. I'll tell you everything when I get home."

Home. I like the sound of that. "Okay. Well, be careful. With everything that's happened, who knows what could come next."

"I will. Hey, Ruby, do me a favor, please?"

"Sure. What is it?"

"Don't let anyone into the apartment while I'm gone, okay? No one. Especially not your dad."

"My dad? He doesn't even know where I am."

"I know, but please don't talk to him or see him unless I'm with you. Please promise me. It's important."

"All right. I promise."

"I'll be home as soon as I can. If you need me, just call, okay?"

"All right."

After we end the call, I sit at my worktable and stare out the window at the skyline in the distance. Miguel didn't sound like himself, not at all. I know there's something he's not telling me.

Pumpkin jumps up in my lap and rubs against me. "Be careful, buddy. No cat hair in the painting."

I push my chair back from the table and cradle Pumpkin for a little one-on-one quality time. "How do you like our new place? Well, our temporary place anyway."

He chirps contentedly.

"You saved my life, you sweet boy." I kiss the top of his head. I don't want to think about what might've happened if he hadn't knocked over my coffee when he did. I'd probably be dead. I shudder at the thought.

I'm feeling a bit restless since Miguel's call, and I'm finding it difficult to concentrate on my work. So, I carry Pumpkin to the living room, and we curl up on the sofa and turn on the TV. I need something to distract me while I'm waiting for Miguel to come back.

Exhaustion creeps up on me, and I end up stretching out on the sofa. Pumpkin curls up in front of me.

The sound of the deadbolt turning wakes me from a fitful sleep. I sit upright, my heart pounding. It takes me a second to orient myself. The room is dark, and the TV is on.

The door opens, and Miguel walks in. "Hey, I'm sorry I'm so late," he says quietly. "I got back as soon as I could. There was a lot going on."

"What's wrong?"

He joins me on the sofa, and Pumpkin climbs into his lap, purring. Miguel looks pensive. He sighs heavily. "I don't even know where to start, Ruby."

"What did you find out?"

"More than I bargained for."

I shift to face him. "What?" I can see the hesitation on his face. "What aren't you telling me, Miguel?"

He looks truly pained, as if he knows what he's about to say is going to hurt me.

"Just start at the beginning. Did you find out who put the drug in my coffee?"

He nods. "Yes. It was Darren," he says with absolute certainty.

I feel gut punched. "What? No!"

"I'm sorry. I know you didn't think he was behind the stalking, but he is."

I sink back against the sofa cushions. "I can't believe it."

Miguel scrubs his hands over his face. "That's just the beginning."

"What else?" I see so much reluctance in his eyes. Whatever it is he knows, it's bad. My pulse starts racing. "Just tell me, Miguel."

He shakes his head in dismay. "Honey, I don't want to do this to you."

"Do what?" Now he's scaring me. "Just say it."

He takes my hands in his and squeezes lightly. "It's hard to know where to start. It took me so long to get back here because I had to wait for Detective Cartwright to arrive at Darren's apartment. Darren made a full confession."

"What did he say?"

"That he put the GHB in your coffee. But in his defense, he swears he didn't know it was enough to do real harm." Miguel pauses, absently rubbing the back of my hands with his thumb. "Someone gave him the GHB and instructed him to put it in your coffee."

"Who?"

Miguel just stares at me, clearly not wanting to say more.

"Who, Miguel? You can tell me."

"Allen."

I can feel the blood drain from my face. My stomach tightens into a knot, and I feel sick. "My dad? That's impossible."

"Darren was arrested tonight. So was Allen. They were both charged with attempted murder. They're in police custody."

I shake my head in disbelief. "My dad? No—that can't be." Tears spring into my eyes. "We had our differences, yes, but I can't believe he would want to hurt me."

Miguel tightens his hold on my hands. "Ruby, Allen's

not your father. Not biologically, anyway."

I pull free from Miguel's grasp and shoot to my feet. I start pacing, all the while shaking my head. "Don't be ridiculous. Of course he's my father."

Miguel stands. "I'm so sorry, honey. I hated having to tell you."

I stop pacing and face him. "I don't understand any of this." Then the obvious question pops into my head. "If my father isn't my biological father, then who is? Am I adopted?"

Miguel shakes his head. "No. You're not adopted. Helen was your biological mother."

"Then who—"

"I think Edward McCall is your biological father."

The room starts spinning then, and I feel light-headed. When I take a step, the floor falls out from under me. Miguel catches me before I hit the ground and sits me down on the sofa. He sits beside me and brushes my hair back from my face. It's not until he starts wiping my cheeks that I realize I'm crying.

"Do you remember telling me about the time your parents split up for a few weeks?" he asks.

I nod.

"During that time, your mom stayed with Edward,

right? It's possible they hooked up. Shortly after your mom reconciled with Allen, she discovered she was pregnant. She told Allen the baby was his. It wasn't until after your mom died that he ordered a paternity test. He had suspected all along that he wasn't your biological father. The paternity test proved it."

"Does Edward know?"

"No, I don't think so."

The implications hit me all at once. "This explains so much. This is why my dad's—Allen's—manner toward me changed so drastically after my mom died. That must be when he found out."

Miguel nods.

"But why didn't he tell me?"

Miguel winces. "Because you're about to inherit a trust fund worth half a billion dollars."

"My dad—Allen—wants my money?"

"I'm afraid so. There's more to it—Allen's been embezzling money from his investment clients for years, and his scheme is about to collapse. He's broke. He needed access to your money to repay his clients before they discover the money is missing."

"And he was willing to kill me to get it?"

"If you died, he'd inherit your assets as your next of

kin."

"But how does Darren come into this?"

"Darren works for Allen. Allen told him to move into your apartment building and befriend you—to keep an eye on you, at first, and report back to him. The initial plan was for Darren to court you and eventually marry you, thereby gaining access to your inheritance. When that failed, Allen switched to Plan B, which was the stalking. Allen thought if they could scare you badly enough, you'd agree to move back home with him. When Edward hired *me* to discover who was stalking you, Allen decided his only option was to end your life and thereby inherit the money himself as your next of kin."

I'm numb. Miguel's speaking, but the words no longer make any sense to me. My mind is spinning, my thoughts roiling. I stand. "This is all too much. I'm going to bed."

As I head to the bathroom, Miguel follows me. I close the door behind me, lock it, and turn on the faucet to splash cold water on my face. When I straighten and stare at my bedraggled reflection, I no longer recognize who I am.

I'm not Ruby Foster.

I'm not who I thought I was.

Now I know why my father seems to hate me. I'm the

result of an affair. As I stare at myself in the mirror, I look for any resemblance between me and Edward, but I really don't see it. Other than having blue eyes, we really don't share any features. I look like my mother—red hair and blue eyes. I have her pale complexion and slender nose. I have her freckles. Her hairline. Her lips. I look so much like my mom that I can't see any resemblance to anyone else.

The bathroom door creaks, giving away the fact that Miguel is leaning against it. Even now, he's protecting me. When fresh tears burn my eyes, I turn on the shower and step into the tub fully dressed. I turn my face into the warm spray and let the water wash away my tears.

I don't want anyone to see me cry.

Not over my father—Allen.

Not over the fact that my life has been a lie.

"Ruby?" Miguel's voice is muffled by the door. He knocks quietly. "Honey, are you okay?"

But I can't answer him. The tears continue to fall, and I can't stop shaking, sobbing.

I hear the door knob jiggle, and then the door opens. I smile. *He picked the lock.*

"Ruby? Are you okay?"

I sigh. "I'm fine."

Miguel peeks around the shower curtain and peers in at me. If he's surprised to see me fully dressed, he doesn't show it. "I was worried about you."

I nod as rivulets of water stream down my face. My soaked clothes hang heavily on my body, weighing me down.

Miguel kicks off his shoes and removes his socks. He digs his wallet out of his back pocket and tosses it onto the counter. Then he steps into the shower with me, fully dressed. He pulls me into his arms and holds me tight. "It's okay," he murmurs into my wet hair. "I've got you. Everything's going to be fine. You'll see."

"Edward's probably my father." Then the sobs increase in intensity. "He's always been there for me, and he doesn't even know I'm his daughter. Do you think he loved my mother?"

"Probably."

"He must have been heartbroken when she died."

Miguel kisses my forehead. "I imagine he was."

"Do I ask him if it's possible?"

"I think you need a good night's sleep before you start making decisions about the future." Miguel reaches around me to shut off the water. Then he grabs a towel from the rack and wraps it around me. "Let's get you into bed, okay?"

I realize I'm standing here in my wet clothes. "Would you mind getting me a nightgown?"

"Of course not." He steps out of the tub and quickly strips out of his wet T-shirt and jeans, until he's left in only his boxer-briefs. He grabs a towel from the linen cupboard and quickly dries himself. "I'll be right back."

While he's gone, I strip out of my wet clothes and re-wrap my body in the bath towel. I step out of the tub and wrap my hair in a towel.

Miguel returns with a pale blue floral nightgown. "Is this okay?"

"Yes, thank you."

He slips the nightgown over my turbaned head, and as he tugs the nightgown down my body, I let the towel fall to the floor.

While I brush my teeth, Miguel opens the vanity drawer and pulls out my comb, which he hands to me. I spit and rinse, then wipe my mouth on a tissue. Once that's all done, I remove the towel from my head and start combing my hair.

"Here, let me," he says, holding out his hand.

I give him my comb and stand in front of the mirror as he carefully untangles my hair. As he works on the long strands, I feel my pulse slowing to a more normal rate. I glance around the bathroom, which seems so familiar with all my things here, and yet it's different. It's a far nicer bathroom than the one in my apartment. The materials and the finishes are new and upscale, unlike the pink wall tiles in my apartment that date back to the forties. This apartment is both familiar and new.

Miguel's reflection in the mirror makes me smile. He's concentrating so hard on my hair—on not hurting me.

When he finishes, he lays the comb on the vanity. "All done." He gathers the damp strands of my hair together, off my shoulders, and lays his hands on my shoulders, squeezing lightly. "You should get some sleep now. There's a lot we have to do tomorrow. Detective Cartwright will need to speak to you, and then you'll need to think about what you're going to tell Edward."

As I meet his gaze in the mirror, I'm overwhelmed with emotion. This man is the most caring—the most nurturing—person I've ever known.

I turn to face him, and he gazes down at me hesitantly. Almost warily. "What is it? Do you need something?"

My breath catches in my throat and butterflies careen inside my belly. *Yes, there's something I need.*

Something I want.

Something I'm afraid to ask for—and yet I'm even more afraid of never having it. I've seen how Miguel looks at me. I remember full well the hunger in his kiss earlier this evening.

He kissed me.

"Would you be terribly upset if I kissed you?" I ask.

His eyes widen. "Ruby." His voice is low, hoarse, suddenly rough with something that sounds like longing.

God, I hope I'm not wrong about this—about his feelings for me—because if I am, I'm about to make a huge fool of myself.

27

Miguel

I stand fixed like a statue, practically holding my breath as Ruby's hand skims up my chest and then slips around to the back of my neck, her fingers soft and cool on my skin. My muscles are locked, my skin feels too tight, and my heart is beating so hard I figure she must be able to hear it.

"Would you be terribly upset if I kissed you?" she asks.

"Ruby." My voice nearly cracks when I say her name. I'm so afraid of misreading the situation. All I can do is shake my head.

She reaches up and draws my face down to hers, and we meet halfway. And then she kisses me. There's no misunderstanding. Her lips are soft and silky and clinging to mine, trembling. She's breathless. And the soft whimpers she's making arouse the hell out of me.

Her lips glide against mine, and she sighs softly. The sound and the light brush of air against my lips sends my body into overdrive. I slip my arms around her torso and pull her close. I know she can feel my body's reaction.

She deepens the kiss, and that's the only cue I need. This woman—this red-haired goddess—is kissing me like she means it.

My conscience raises its ugly head, making me take a step back. "Ruby, are you sure? You've had a major shock tonight."

"I'm sure," she says.

She gazes up at me with those crystalline blue eyes. I don't see fear in her eyes, or hesitation—I see need. I see desire. I scoop her up in my arms and carry her across the hall to her bedroom. I nudge the door open and carry her inside. Pumpkin races into her bedroom ahead of us and jumps up on the bed.

I sit Ruby on the bed and grab the cat. "Not right now,

pal. We're kind of in the middle of something." He's still purring when I deposit him on the floor outside her bedroom and close the door.

"Miguel?"

"Yes?"

"Um, do you have protection on you?"

"Yes. I always carry something in my wallet."

She laughs nervously. "Good, because I don't. And I'm not on the pill. Is that a problem? I hope it's not a problem." She looks so nervous, so unprepared.

"Oh, sweetheart." I crouch down beside the bed and lay my hands on her thighs. Her nightgown has ridden up almost to her panty line, only I happen to know she's not wearing any panties right now. My dick twitches as I start to harden. "Of course it's not a problem. Are you sure you're ready for this?" I can't afford to mess this up.

She nods, looking somewhat relieved. "Yes, I'm sure." She lays her hands on mine. "I want to be with you, Miguel. I mean, if you want that, too."

I swallow hard. "Yes, I want that, too." My voice sounds rough. "I do." I stand up. "I'll be right back." I run to the bathroom to grab my wallet, double-checking that I do indeed have a condom with me. *Thank God, I do.*

When I return to the bedroom, I find Ruby sitting

nervously at the side of the bed, her hands clasped in her lap.

Then it dawns on me. *She's a virgin.*

"You've never done this before, have you?" I realize what a huge step this is for her—to trust me like this. To allow me to be her first.

Her first.

But I want to be more than her first. I want to be *her only.*

Slow down, I tell myself. *Don't scare her.*

She shakes her head. "No. Never." She squeezes my hand. "But I want this, with you."

My mind is racing. *Go slow, don't rush her, ease her into it. Make it good for her.*

I kneel on the bed, looming over her, supporting myself on one hand while the other slides into her hair. The long strands fan out around her, like a halo of fire. *God, she's beautiful.* I lean down to trail nibbling kisses along her neck, skimming lightly, teasing her. I smile when she shivers.

Take it slow.

I press my mouth to her pulse point and suck gently, although I'm careful not to leave a mark.

Not too fast.

I skim my lips upward to trail kisses along her jawline, up the side of her cheek to the sensitive spot behind her ear. She shivers.

My God, she's so responsive.

More light kisses up to her temple, her forehead, and when she closes her eyes, I feather soft kisses on her eyelids.

Her hands latch tightly onto my arms. Then, and only then, do I allow myself to capture her mouth. Her lips part on a breathy sigh, and I deepen the kiss. I nudge her lips open wider and touch the tip of my tongue to hers. She startles a moment at the unfamiliar touch, but then she eases into it, stroking my tongue with hers.

She's going to be the death of me.

Ruby releases my arms and slides her hands over my chest, stroking my heated skin. Her palms travel up to my shoulders, and she clutches them.

Slow, slow, slow... it's like a mantra in my head. A reminder not to rush her.

Ease her into it.

But then she surprises me when she skims her soft fingers down my chest to my abs. She brushes the line of hair that runs from my navel to disappear beneath the waistband of my briefs. *Oh, fuck!*

Okay, it's time to lose our clothes. I lean back and grasp the hem of her nightgown. "Let's take this off, all right?" I wait for her to nod before I slowly start to lift it. She raises her hips, then sits up as I drag the garment up past her belly, then her waist, and finally to her breasts. My gaze fixes on her breasts—perfect little mounds of cream-colored flesh topped with pink nipples. Right before my eyes, those nipples begin to tighten into little buds. When I brush one nipple lightly with the tip of my index finger, she gasps.

I pull the nightgown off her and toss it aside. Her arms come up and cross over her chest, covering her breasts. She looks so nervous, so unsure.

"We can stop if you want to," I tell her. "We don't have to do this tonight. There's no rush. We can take our time."

"No!" She laughs at her own outburst. "I mean, no, that's okay. I don't want to wait. I'm nervous, that's all. I don't want to mess this up."

I chuckle. "Honey, that's *my* line."

"I don't want to make a fool of myself."

"Ruby, if anyone's going to do that, it'll be me."

She smiles. "You're just being nice."

"No, I'm being truthful."

She drops her arms to her side then, revealing herself. I want to devour her. I'm desperate to go down on her, but I'm afraid that might be too much for her first time. There are other ways I can make her feel good.

I urge her to scoot across the bed, and I follow her. I lie beside her and kiss her sensitive throat. I already know she likes that. My hand skims down to her chest, and I cover one of her breasts, molding it to fit my palm. I brush her nipple gently, teasing the tight little bud, and she cries out. And while I'm keeping her occupied with my mouth on first one nipple, then the other, I slip my other hand down her soft belly to the sweet spot between her thighs.

When I touch her, she arches her hips and gasps, "Miguel!"

Hearing her say my name like that blows my mind. "Trust me, sweetheart. I'll make this good for you, I swear."

28

Ruby

I'm so nervous I can barely breathe. I'm lying here completely naked. It's nerve-racking. No one has ever seen me naked before. But the hunger in Miguel's dark eyes gives me some desperately needed confidence.

This is really happening.

He's *touching* me, his fingers gentle and searching, skimming and teasing. His fingers glide easily through my slick arousal. At least my body knows what to do.

When his finger glances over my clitoris, a shiver

courses through me. Then his thumb is there, and he starts rubbing gentle circles over the sensitive flesh, alternating the pressure. He eases my legs farther apart, and then his finger is exploring my opening, probing gently.

When he slips his finger inside me, I suck in a shocked breath.

"Okay?" he asks, and then he kisses me. His lips are soft and coaxing on mine.

"Mm-hmm." I'm past the ability to make coherent speech.

He chuckles. "You can tell me to stop at any time. If you change your mind—"

"No! Don't you dare stop."

He laughs softly as he kisses me. His thumb teases my clitoris relentlessly, distracting me as his finger sinks deeper and deeper. I feel a stretch and a slight burn, but nothing painful. It feels... good. It feels right. Like this is meant to be.

I run my hands up his arms, marveling at how firm his muscles are, like stones beneath his warm skin. I grasp his shoulders, holding on to steady myself.

His finger starts to move easily inside me, sliding in and out. Then he sinks it deeper, and I gasp at the feeling of fullness. He focuses on a spot inside, rubbing gently, but persistently, and soon I feel a tingling warmth blossoming deep inside me.

He pulls back, and we stare into each other's eyes, our gazes locked.

"You are so beautiful," he whispers. "*Cariño.*"

"What does that mean?"

He smiles down at me. "It means, 'sweetheart or love.'"

He trails kisses across my cheeks, then smiles at me. "I've wanted to kiss your freckles since the moment we met." Then he presses his lips to mine, kissing me sweetly.

When he suddenly rises up and off the bed, I'm about to protest when I realize he's shoving his briefs down his long legs. *Oh, my.*

My gaze latches onto his impressive erection.

That's a whole lot bigger than his finger.

He smiles. "Don't worry."

"That's easy for you to say."

After he kicks off his underwear, he grabs the condom packet off the nightstand and tears it open. He sheathes himself quickly, and then he's back on the bed, kneeling between my thighs. His warm hand skims past my hip to my knee, and he nudges my legs apart so he can rest between them.

He leans down and kisses me, his lips soft and coaxing. He trails kisses down my throat to my chest.

I'm trembling when I watch him take hold of his erection and guide it to my opening. My pulse races, and I close my eyes.

"Ruby."

I look up to find him gazing down at me.

"It's okay, honey. Just keep your eyes on me." And then he moves forward, slowly sinking into me.

There's pressure and a slight stretching and burn, and then with a little bit of a determined push, he slides into me. I stiffen in surprise at the sudden sting, a pinching feeling, but then it eases just as quickly.

He lowers his mouth to mine and gently teases my lips. "It's okay," he murmurs. "I'm in. The worst is over."

My muscles are tense, but when he starts to move, gliding in and out, I realize he's right. This feels... good. There's no pain, just a delicious fullness. He moves easily now, so slowly, and my body melts.

He kisses me again, drinking in my sighs and all the surprising sounds coming from me. I find myself making sounds I've never made before.

He thrusts slowly, gradually building speed. His

thumb works my clit, rubbing tiny circles, alternating between firm and soft touches. My body tingles from head to toe as pleasure swells inside me, starting low in my belly, then radiating outward. My muscles tense suddenly as a wave of pleasure sweeps through me, stealing my breath.

He bucks into me, his cries low and rough. When my body clamps down on him, he arches his back, crying out hoarsely as he sinks deep inside me, holding himself there as his muscles lock tight and his erection throbs inside me.

I glance at his expression, tense now, his jaws clenched. His gaze latches onto mine, and I'm shocked by the vulnerability I see in his beautiful obsidian eyes. This means something to him, just as it does to me.

Still inside me Miguel rolls us gently onto our sides. "You okay?" he asks a bit breathlessly.

I nod. "I'm wonderful."

He kisses my forehead. "Yes, you are."

* * *

After Miguel disposes of the condom and we clean up in the bathroom, Miguel scoops me into his arms and carries me back to my bed and lays me down.

"Will you stay with me?" I ask.

He smiles. "Wild horses couldn't drag me away."

Pumpkin jumps up onto the bed, climbing over us and purring loudly.

Miguel turns me on my side and presses up close behind me. He wraps his arms around my waist and tucks me in close.

For the first time all evening, I can finally relax. My body is thrumming, and I feel a delicious, if unfamiliar, ache deep inside.

I lost my virginity tonight. It's as surprising as it is wonderful. I never expected this to happen. I never dreamed I could ever trust someone this much. I've never even met someone who made me want to try. With Miguel, everything feels different. I feel different. Stronger.

I clasp Miguel's arm to my chest. He makes me feel safe—something no one has ever done before. He also gives me strength to deal with what comes next.

Tomorrow is going to be difficult—I know that. I'll have to face all the things Miguel told me this evening, about my father—I mean Allen. I keep thinking of him as my father, but this is a man who was willing to kill me to get what he wanted.

And then there's Edward. How is Edward going to react when he finds out he might be my father? We have a great relationship, and he's always been there for me, but finding out he's possibly my father might be a shock.

And then there's the police detective. I know he's going to come asking questions, and I dread that.

"Are you okay?" Miguel whispers close to my ear, his breath ruffling my hair.

I shiver. "Yes. I'm just thinking about tomorrow."

He tightens his arm around my waist. "There's nothing to worry about. I'll be with you every step of the way."

"I'm going to call Edward tomorrow and ask him to come over. He needs to know the truth."

"I don't think you need to worry about Edward. I have a feeling he's going to be thrilled to welcome you as his daughter."

29

Miguel

Detective Cartwright arrives at the apartment at ten the next morning. Ruby's been a nervous wreck since we woke up, and she's hiding in her art studio when Cartwright knocks on our door.

I let the man in. He's dressed in a rumpled navy blue suit.

"It looks like you had a rough night," I say.

Cartwright nods. "After interviewing the two suspects last night, taking their statements, I started putting together a timeline of events."

"Are they still in custody?"

The detective nods. "Yes, both of them. They'll be arraigned soon, probably tomorrow. I expect Darren will be released on bail. He's been rather cooperative. I'm not sure about Allen Foster. He's not cooperating. I'd consider him a flight risk given the financial mismanagement charges he's facing in addition to a charge of attempted murder."

Cartwright glances around the living room. "Can I speak to Miss Foster?"

I nod. "She's expecting you. I'll go get her. Just take it easy with her, will you? She's had a rough time of it."

I filled him in on her agoraphobia last night, and he seems pretty sympathetic, especially after what Ruby's been through.

I head down the hallway and knock on her studio door. "Ruby, honey? Can I come in?"

"Yes." Her voice is muffled.

I open the door and find her sitting at her worktable. She has a paintbrush in hand, and she's working on a painting of a gray tabby cat. "He's here. Are you ready to talk to him?"

She sighs. "Yes." She slips her paintbrush into a jar of

water, pushes her chair back from the table, and stands. "I might as well get this over with."

I offer her my hand, wanting to show my support. She takes it with a forced smile, and we walk together out to the living room.

Ruby studies the middle-aged man seated on the chair beside the sofa. He has a notebook in hand, as well as a pen. When he spots us, he sets them on the coffee table and stands.

"Good morning, Miss Foster," he says. "Thanks for agreeing to see me. I promise not to keep you longer than necessary."

Ruby smiles perfunctorily. It's not like she has a choice in the matter.

She and I sit on the sofa, hands clasped. I intentionally place myself between Ruby and Cartwright, hoping that will make her feel more secure with me as a buffer between them.

"Let me start off saying I'm sorry about what you've been through," the man says to Ruby. "I'm glad you're all right."

"Thanks," she says.

I squeeze her hand.

"I assume Miguel filled you in on what we discovered

last night," the detective says.

She nods. "He did."

The detective summarizes what happened last night, what Darren revealed to me, what he's confessed to. How Allen Foster was apprehended and questioned. "Both men are in police custody at the moment, pending arraignment."

Ruby simply nods.

"Your father's apartment was searched last night," Cartwright continues. "We found a supply of the drug he directed Darren Ingles to put into your coffee. This morning, a financial forensic team raided your father's office and confiscated his computers and documents that show the money he stole from his clients. The preliminary evidence seems pretty cut and dry, and based on previous similar cases, it looks like Mr. Foster is going to spend a long time in a federal prison."

"What about Darren?" Ruby asks.

"Darren is cooperating with law enforcement and with prosecutors, so that will benefit him when it comes to sentencing. I think he genuinely regrets the role he played in your father's scheme."

Ruby tightens her grip on my hand. "Allen Foster isn't my father."

Cartwright winces. "That's right. I'm sorry."

After Cartwright takes Ruby's statement about what happened the night she was drugged, he thanks her and stands to leave. While I walk him to the door, Ruby remains seated on the sofa, seemingly numb after hearing all over again that Allen Foster—the man she knew as her father—had attempted to kill her.

After Cartwright's gone, I return to the sofa and sit beside her, putting my arm around her. She melts into me. "I'm so sorry, Ruby."

She presses her face against my shoulder but doesn't say anything.

"What next? Do you want to talk to Edward? He should know what Allen's done. He should also know that Allen's not your biological father, and that we think he is."

She nods. "Yes, we need to tell him." She sounds so defeated.

"What's wrong? What are you afraid of?"

"What if he doesn't want a father-daughter relationship with me?"

"What if he does? What if he's thrilled to learn he's your biological father? What if he jumps at the chance to have a relationship with you?"

She nods. "Would you call him, please?"

I call Edward and ask him to come to the new apartment. "Ruby needs to talk to you."

"Of course!" he says. "I'll be over as soon as I can. Give me half an hour, tops, okay?"

When I end the call, I lean close and kiss her temple. "I have a feeling you'll be pleasantly surprised by Edward's reaction. I've seen how he is when he talks about you. It's obvious he cares for you very deeply."

"This might change everything."

* * *

Ruby flinches when there's a knock at our door. We're still sitting on the sofa—we haven't moved since Cartwright left. I think Ruby's still processing everything the detective told her. And now we're going to have to relive it all over again when we explain things to Edward.

I let Edward in. We shake hands, and then his gaze goes right to Ruby. "How are you feeling, kiddo?" he asks.

When she just stares at him without answering, he loses his smile. "What's wrong?"

He crosses the room to sit beside her on the sofa. I sit on her other side.

"Ruby?" Edward asks as he puts his arm around her and draws her close. "What's wrong, sweetheart?"

Ruby looks to me to fill him in, so I give him the breakdown of what has transpired since last night. I tell him about Allen's plot to terrorize Ruby, Darren's involvement, and that Allen and Darren have both been arrested for attempted murder. By the time I'm done, he looks like a man in shock.

Edward shakes his head. "I can't believe it. How could Allen—it doesn't make sense. Oh, sweetheart, I'm so sorry. How could a father do that to his own daughter?"

"He's not my father." Ruby blurts out the words.

Looking shellshocked, Edward glances at me. "What?"

I nod. "It's true. Allen had a paternity test done years ago. He's not her biological father. She just found out last night."

I tell Edward the rest—that Allen had doubts that Ruby was his biological child, and that after Helen died, Allen had a paternity test performed to confirm his suspicions.

It's pretty clear from the look on Edward's face that he knew nothing about any of this.

Ruby reaches for Edward's hand. "Is it possible you're my father?"

Edward's eyes widen. "Yes, it's possible," he says, confirming our suspicions that he and Helen had a brief affair while she was separated from Allen.

"To be honest," he says, "I did wonder about the timing of Helen's pregnancy. I knew it was possible the baby could be mine. But when she never said anything to me about it, and she reconciled with Allen, I assumed I was mistaken. That it must have been wishful thinking on my part."

Edward reaches out and cups Ruby's cheek. "I've always loved you like you were my own child. You were Helen's child, and that was enough for me. I couldn't have loved you more if I'd known you were mine." He sighs. "Do you—" He stops abruptly, clearly choked up. "Ruby, would you want a relationship with me? Will you let me be your father and make up for all that lost time?"

When she nods, Edward pulls her into his arms. The two of them cling to each other, both overwhelmed with emotion.

Ruby's quiet sobs are tearing me up.

Edward pats her back and reassures her. "It's all right, sweetheart." He kisses the top of her head. "I'm just sorry we didn't find out sooner."

When they finally release each other, Edward sits back

looking stunned. "I'm a father," he muses. "I have a family." Then he looks at me. "How about that, Miguel? I'm a father." His shock quickly gives way to astonishment and then to joy.

"Ever since Mom died, I felt like Allen resented me—even hated me," Ruby tells Edward. "Our relationship was never the same after we lost Mom. Now I know why. I thought he blamed me for her death, but it wasn't that. He resented me because I was proof that she'd been with someone else."

"I should have pressed Helen," Edward says. "I just thought it was wishful thinking on my part, thinking you could have been mine. When she never said a word, I let it go. She seemed happy back with Allen again, and I didn't want to mess that up for her. And when she asked me to be your godfather, I was thrilled. Of course, I said yes. At least this way I could be part of your life."

Ruby invites Edward to stay for lunch. I run out to my uncle's restaurant and pick up food for the three of us and bring it back. We sit outside on the balcony to eat tacos and tamales, and we toast to Edward and Ruby's new relationship with ice-cold bottles of Corona. I even allow myself to drink one beer since Ruby and I don't have any plans to go anywhere anytime soon.

Ruby seems more at ease now than I've ever seen her. The threat of her stalker is gone, and Edward knows the truth. And even though she's been through a lot of trauma recently, she's coming out of this with a new relationship with a man who's beyond overjoyed to find out he's likely her father.

When we're done eating, I take the dishes to the kitchen and clean up. I want to give the father and daughter some time alone. After all the recent heartache Ruby's experienced, I think this new relationship with Edward is just what she needs. Now she has a father who adores her, not one who ridicules her and makes her feel unloved.

When Edward leaves to head back to his office, Ruby walks him to the door. Edward gives her a bear hug, and the two of them hold each other for a good long time. I have a feeling we'll be seeing a lot more of Edward now.

After he's gone, she locks the door, then turns to me with a bright smile on her face.

"I told you he'd be thrilled," I tell her. "He's the one who hired McIntyre Security to protect you. It wasn't Allen. It was Edward. Even without knowing the truth, Edward was more of a father to you than Allen was."

30

Ruby

After Edward leaves, I return to my art studio to try to catch up on my current commissions. I have several paintings that are ready to be varnished. As soon as they dry, I'll package them up for shipping. I'll need to talk to Miguel about shipping. There must be a mailroom in the building.

As I'm prepping a few canvases for new projects, Miguel knocks on my open door. "You busy?"

I glance up from my worktable. "No. Just getting some

new canvases ready."

"Jason just texted. He and Layla would like to come over this evening to welcome you to the building. They've offered to bring dinner. Are you okay with having some company?"

"Jason and Layla? Sure." They're both nice, and I need to start making friends. If I want any type of *normalcy*, I need to move past my comfort zone, and that includes making friends.

"Is pizza okay? They've offered to pick up some pizzas."

"Sure. I'll never turn down a pizza."

"Margherita?"

"Yes. That sounds great."

* * *

When we hear a knock, Miguel answers the door. I rush to the bathroom to freshen up and brush my hair. When I join them in the living room, I see three pizza boxes spread out on the coffee table, along with bottles of Coke and water. Layla's sitting in the armchair, and Jason's sitting on the floor at her feet. They left the sofa for me and Miguel.

"Hi, guys," I say, standing just in the living room. I try

my best to ignore my racing pulse. *It's okay. These people are friends.*

Layla stands and holds out a bouquet of fresh-cut wildflowers wrapped in plastic. "These are for you." She gives me a hug. "Welcome to the building."

"Thank you," I say as she hands them to me. "They're gorgeous."

Layla glances around the apartment, at all the plants hanging by the balcony doors and the potted trees and plants out on the balcony. "I'm glad your plants made the move, too."

"Thanks to Miguel, everything made it over here. It feels just like home, only everything's newer and shinier. And we have more space."

We. Like we share this apartment. Like it's *ours.*

I have to keep reminding myself this is only temporary. And now that Miguel uncovered who was stalking me—and why—I suppose our arrangement is going to come to an end soon. Miguel was hired to assess my situation. Not only did he assess it, but he also uncovered the culprits—Darren and Allen. I'm trying to get used to thinking of Allen as *Allen*, and not as my dad.

"I'll get us some plates and napkins," Miguel says as he heads for the kitchen.

I gaze at the beautiful bouquet of flowers. "I'll go put these in water." I follow Miguel into the kitchen and pull a glass vase out from underneath the sink.

"That was nice of Layla to bring you a housewarming gift," Miguel says as I fill the vase with water.

"It is." As I unwrap the bouquet and set it in the vase, I realize this is my first housewarming gift. And I think Layla is my first friend. There have been so many firsts lately, my head is spinning. Little by little, I'm inching toward the kind of life I want.

I arrange the stems in the vase and stand back to look at the result. "What do you think?" I ask Miguel.

He leans close and kisses my cheek. "I think it's perfect."

I set the vase in the center of the kitchen table. Then I join the others in the living room, where Miguel is handing out plates and napkins. Everyone grabs a slice of pizza and a drink.

"Mmm," I say, moaning when I take my first bite. "I haven't had pizza this good in *years*."

"Hey," Miguel says, elbowing me playfully. "I think your homemade pizza is as good as this."

I laugh. "You're just being nice."

"No, I'm serious," he says. He leans close and kisses

the side of my head. "In fact, I think your pizza is better."

"Liar," I say. I can't help smiling, though. His praise means the world to me.

As everyone starts to dig in to their food, I notice Jason subtly using his phone to read the glucose monitor on Layla's arm. It dawns on me—he's not just her boyfriend. He's also her—what? Her protector? Like Miguel has been for me. But clearly they live together as a couple—as a romantic couple. I sneak a peek at Miguel and find him watching me with a curious expression on his face. It's almost a longing, and I wonder if he's thinking the same thing I am.

I would give anything for Miguel to remain in my life once this is all over. I suppose I could hire him to stay with me—as my protector. My twenty-fifth birthday is next month. I'll inherit my trust fund, and then money won't be a problem.

After we finish eating, Layla helps me carry the dirty dishes to the kitchen. As I rinse them off and put them in the dishwasher—I finally have a dishwasher!—she leans against the counter.

"How do you like the apartment?" she asks.

"I love it. It's much nicer than my apartment."

I try not to stare at Layla, but it's hard. She's stunning,

with her silky straight black hair and dark eyes lined in kohl. I'm not sure what her ethnic background is, but I'm guessing Middle Eastern or Mediterranean. She's wearing a short-sleeve, knit tunic with gray leggings and a pair of short black boots. The logo on the tunic is from University of Chicago.

I point at her outfit. "You go to University of Chicago?"

She nods. "I'm a sophomore."

"What's your major?"

"Psychology. I'd like to be a mental health counselor."

"Wow, that's admirable."

She shrugs. "I have a lot of experience when it comes to counseling. I've been helped by some great counselors, so I thought maybe I could help others."

"I guess we have that in common. I've been in counseling on and off since—well, for years. You know, for agoraphobia."

Layla gives me a small smile. "Me too, but for auditory hallucinations."

Her admission takes me by surprise. "Auditory hallucinations?" It takes a moment for that to sink in. "You hear things?"

"Yes. Voices—mean girl voices. At least that's how I characterize them." She laughs. "So if I zone out on you, please don't take it personally. Sometimes they're very distracting. It can be hard to block them out."

"Do you hear them all the time?"

She frowns. "Not all the time, but often."

Her ear buds are starting to make sense now. "So that's why you listen to music a lot?"

She nods. "It helps me focus."

I feel a sudden kinship with Layla, that we have more in common than I realized. "It looks like we both have challenges."

Layla nods. "Yep. I just thought you'd want to know you're not the only one dealing with issues. It's a lot easier for me, now, with Jason in my life. He always seems to know what I need."

"Is he—" I break off here, not sure what to ask. "Are you guys—"

She smiles. "He's my boyfriend, yes, but he's also my bodyguard. He monitors my health."

"When we were eating I noticed Jason checking your blood sugar."

"I'm a type 1 diabetic. Let's just say I keep Jason on his toes."

As we finish cleaning up the kitchen, Layla says, "You know, I've known Miguel for a while now. He and Jason are close. Miguel's also good friends with my brother, Ian."

"It's a small world, isn't it?"

"Yes, but my point is, everyone likes Miguel. He's a great guy."

I feel my cheeks heating. "Yes, he is." If I'm not mistaken, I think Layla's doing a bit of matchmaking.

Miguel pops his head through the kitchen doorway. "We found one of Liam's championship fights on YouTube. You girls want to come watch it with us?"

"Sure," Layla says. "Come on." She gestures for me to follow. "Liam teaches martial arts and self-defense at McIntyre Security. He's also a champion MMA fighter."

We return to the living room and get comfortable watching Liam McIntyre dominate his opponent in a boxing ring. Honestly, it's a bit brutal to watch. I find myself flinching every time he gets hit or kicked.

Liam's championship video leads to another and another.

Miguel stands. "Who wants popcorn? This definitely calls for popcorn."

* * *

Later that evening, after Layla and Jason have gone, Miguel and I are sitting together on the sofa, our feet propped up on the coffee table, in just our socks. We're just chilling.

As my eyes grow heavy, I decide to get ready for bed. I disappear into the bathroom to wash up, and then into my bedroom to change into my nightgown. When I return to the living room, I find that Miguel has changed into a pair of navy-blue-and-white plaid flannel PJ bottoms and a navy blue T-shirt.

Miguel turns off the TV. "Ready for bed?"

"Yes."

We've never really talked about our sleeping arrangement here. He slept with me last night, but I don't know if he plans to do that again, or even if he wants to. I don't want to make any assumptions. He has his own bedroom here. Maybe he wants his own space.

"What's wrong?" he asks.

"Nothing. I just—I was wondering—"

He rises from the sofa and walks up to me with open arms. "Wondering what?"

"About the sleeping arrangements. I mean, are we—" My voice trails off. I don't know how to say this. I've never been in a situation like this.

Miguel sweeps me up into his arms, carries me to my bed, and sets me on my feet. When Pumpkin races into the room and jumps up on the bed, Miguel laughs. "It looks like Pumpkin's already made himself at home."

I don't know the correct etiquette for asking your—what? *bodyguard? roommate?* —if he wants to sleep with you. I sit on the side of the bed and reach for his hand. "Are you sleeping with me tonight?"

He glances down at me, his dark eyes smoldering. "I'd like to, but I didn't want to be presumptuous."

I tug on his hand, drawing him closer. "I'm totally okay with you being presumptuous."

He smiles as he lays me back on the bed. When he kisses me, my whole body heats up. My breasts feel full, and the spot between my legs begins to ache. He links his fingers with mine, holding my hands pinned to the mattress as he comes up over me.

As I gaze up into his dark eyes, I lose myself in their depths. His hands tighten on mine, and I'm so aware of his strength, his passion. He kisses me hungrily, his lips nudging mine open. My pulse races in anticipation.

"How do you feel?" he asks as he slides a hand between my thighs. "You're not sore?"

I know what he's asking. Am I sore from last night?

From losing my virginity? "No. I feel perfect."

As he kisses me, he brings one of my hands down between us. I gasp when I feel his erection brush against the back of my fingers. Releasing his hand, I wrap my fingers around him. He sucks in a breath as I tighten my grip. I'm amazed by how velvety soft his skin is, and yet beneath he's hard as steel.

Without a word, he shows me how to stroke him. I revel in touching him, loving the fact that I'm giving him pleasure. He kisses me hungrily once more, his breathing heavy. I love the sounds he's making. Before long, he covers my hand with his and gently peels my fingers off him. He chuckles roughly. "Much more of that and this'll be over before it begins."

Miguel suddenly moves lower in the bed and nudges my legs again. The next thing I know, he's settled between my thighs. His fingers touch me lightly, spreading me open. When I feel his breath on my heated flesh, I gasp. His tongue flicks my sensitive clitoris, and I cry out, raising my hips up off the bed.

Holy cow, I never dreamed—"Miguel!"

As he torments my clit, his long finger slips carefully inside me, searching and teasing. When he strokes me deep inside, my thighs start trembling. Heat and electricity radiate outward from my core, and my nipples tighten in response. Pleasure explodes inside me, stealing my breath.

Miguel rises up, grabs a condom from the nightstand drawer, and quickly sheaths himself. Every inch of me is still tingling when he guides himself into me. He sinks slowly, all the way, and we both gasp.

"Okay?" he asks, his voice hoarse.

"Yes."

He moves then, slowly at first, almost pulling out before sinking deeply back inside. The friction slowly builds, along with the pleasure. He picks up his pace, and soon he's thrusting hard and fast. Suddenly, he sinks deep and holds himself there. I can feel his erection throbbing inside me. With a rough cry, he arches his back. His expression tightens into a grimace, his jaws clenched.

Miguel rolls us onto our sides. He brushes my hair back from my face before he leans close to kiss me. We're both breathing hard, both of us reeling from the pleasure.

After he disposes of the condom, I visit the bathroom before turning to bed. Miguel pulls me down beside him. The heat of his body sinks into my bones and feels so incredibly good I don't ever want to move.

My fingers intertwine with his. His slow, steady breath ruffles my hair and sends a shiver down my spine. My breasts still feel tight and full, and my nipples are tingling. And best of all, my heart feels full to bursting.

I've never felt this way about anyone before. I never even dreamed this could happen for me. I was locked in my own private world until Miguel came and set me free.

In the short time I've known him, Miguel has given me the things I want and need and dream of… namely security and safety. Because of him, I've met new people—nice people I like. Thanks to him, I've had more of a normal life in the past few days than I've had in years. And I can't help wanting more of the same.

31

Miguel

Ruby's lying with her head on my shoulder, her arm across my waist. We're enjoying a quiet moment in bed, just the two of us. Well, plus Pumpkin. Even he's quiet at the moment.

"I've been thinking," Ruby says.

"What about?"

"My birth certificate. It states that Allen Foster is my birth father. Since that's not true, I want to change it. I was thinking I'd ask Edward if he'd agree to a paternity test, to verify that he's my father. Assuming he is, I'd have his name put on my birth certificate. And maybe I'd change my name to Ruby McCall. I also need a will. If something happens to me, my inheritance should go to Edward, not to Allen Foster."

I tuck a few loose strands of Ruby's hair behind her ear. "I'm sure Edward would be happy to have a paternity test. And if you need a lawyer, I've got a good one to recommend. Troy Spencer—he's the attorney for McIntyre Security. He's also Shane's personal attorney."

"So, what comes next?" she asks.

"What do you mean?"

"Well, now that we know who was doing the stalking, I guess the threat is over."

"Not so fast, I'm afraid. Darren and Allen will undoubtedly get out on bail, and we're not a hundred percent sure there's no one else involved. I think it's too soon to let our guard down. I'd like to stay on your security detail until we're sure."

Ruby leans up on her elbows so she can look me in the eye. "I'm okay with that. In fact, there's something I want to ask you."

"Anything. Just name it."

She grins. "Hold on. You might want to wait until you

hear my idea before you agree to it."

"Okay, shoot."

"Well, I was wondering what you might think about staying on with me indefinitely—in a security capacity, of course. Like Jason does for Layla. When I inherit my trust fund, I'll certainly be able to afford it."

I chuckle. "You could afford an entire army of protectors."

She smiles, displaying dimples. "I don't need a whole army. I think one will be plenty—as long as he's the right one."

"Oh? Do you have someone in mind?"

"I do." She leans forward and presses a light kiss to my lips. "Will you stay?"

I nod, feeling a bit choked up. "I'll gladly stay as long as you need me." *Or forever, if you just say the word.*

* * *

The rest of the week passes pretty quietly. Ruby makes arrangements for a paternity test at a local DNA laboratory. Edward goes in to give a DNA sample, and a visiting nurse comes to the apartment to get Ruby's DNA. They say they'll have the results in two to three days. Ruby's excited, but she's also a bit nervous.

"What if it comes back negative?" she asks me.

"Let's just wait and see what the results are. You'll know for sure very soon."

Ruby finishes up several customer commissions and packages them up for shipping.

I offer to take them down to the mailroom for her. "Would you like to come downstairs with me to check out the mailroom?"

Her eyes widen, and she shakes her head. "No, that's okay."

"All right. I just thought I'd ask."

Later that afternoon, I pop into the art studio to ask if she's ready for some lunch. I glance down at the new painting she's working on and recognize my grandmother's tiny Chihuahua, Sugar. The little cream puff in the painting looks exactly like the real thing.

"That's incredible," I say. I shake my head in disbelief. "How do you do that? I can't even draw stick people."

She shrugs. "I don't know. I see the image in my head and my hand recreates it on canvas."

"*Mi abuelita* is going to love it. Her birthday is in a couple of weeks. Is it okay if I invite her over once it's done, so we can give it to her together?"

Ruby hesitates only a moment before she says, "Yes. I'd love to meet her."

* * *

Two days after both Ruby's and Edward's DNA were submitted to the lab, Ruby receives an e-mail with the results.

"Miguel!"

I'm in the kitchen making our lunch when I hear her call my name. I head to the art studio, where I find her sitting at her desk looking at her computer screen. "What is it?"

"I have an e-mail from the DNA lab."

"Have you opened it?"

She shakes her head. "No, I'm too nervous." She rolls her desk chair back a couple of feet from her desk. "You read it."

I stand behind her chair and gaze down at her monitor. "Are you sure?"

"Yes. I can't stand the suspense. Tell me what it says."

Leaning over her, I open the e-mail and scan the contents. "The results say it's 99% likely that Edward McCall is your biological father. So, yes."

She shoots out of her chair and throws herself into my arms. "Oh, thank God. I wanted him to be my father. I have to call him!"

Ruby grabs her phone and calls Edward. "The paternity results are in. They say it's 99% likely that you're my biological father." She listens for a moment, then says, "Yes! So am I."

I can hear that Edward's talking, but I can't make out the words. I just watch the smile on Ruby's face grow bigger and bigger, and eventually her eyes tear up.

"I'd like that," she says. "How about six?" Then she looks at me and mouths, "He's coming tonight for dinner so we can celebrate."

* * *

When Edward arrives that evening, Ruby greets him at the door. "Hi, Dad," she says, grinning at him.

He throws his arms around her and hugs her tightly. "Hello, daughter."

They both tear up.

Dinner is low key. Ruby and I make pasta and marinara sauce, and we serve it with garlic bread and salad. The three of us eat at the little table in the kitchen. Edward regales Ruby with stories about his most fond memories when she was little. These stories, some of which she'd never heard before, and all of them including her mother, put a smile on her face.

As I sit back and watch the two of them connecting in a way they never have before, I see Ruby blossoming before my eyes. She finally has a parent who loves her, who will gladly give her the affection and validation she didn't get from Allen.

No one mentions Allen or Darren. We're all looking forward to the future.

32

Ruby

"Good morning, sleepyhead," Miguel says.

I open my eyes to a light-filled room. The curtains are open, the sun is shining, and the sky is a clear blue. I consult the wall clock and groan. "It's only eight."

"How'd you sleep?"

"I slept well, thank you."

We have breakfast on the balcony, watching the view across Lake Shore Drive. It's a beautiful day out, and lots of people are taking advantage of the weather and enjoying their time on the water. Boats are flying across the horizon, left to right, right to left. The beach is filled with people.

Miguel reaches for my hand. "What are you thinking about?"

I turn to him. "Just how much I loved visiting the lake with my mom. We'd make a whole day of it. She'd sit on her beach chair and read a book while I built sandcastles and played in the surf. I miss that. I miss being by the water, all the noises, all the excitement."

"Why don't we go?" he asks.

My heart stutters. "Go to the beach?" He makes it sound so easy.

"Sure. It's only two blocks away. Let's go."

* * *

"Are you ready?" Miguel asks me.

I nod. *No.*

He unlocks our door and opens it, then reaches for my hand. He links our fingers together and leads me out of our apartment. I stand frozen while he closes our door and locks it.

"It's okay," he says as he puts an arm around me.

I know he can feel me shaking. I feel sick, queasy. My pulse is racing. *I can't do this.* He thinks I can, but I can't. It's too far away. The space is too open. It's not safe. Anyone could be out there.

I stand rooted to the spot, and Miguel waits patiently beside me. He's not pressuring me. He's not pushing. Just waiting.

"I'll be with you every step," he says. "I promise I'll keep you safe."

I close my eyes and focus on breathing. I picture the lake, the water ebbing and flowing, the water splashing on the beach. Boats in the distance. Sailboats, yachts. Seagulls soaring through the sky.

Miguel pulls me closer, wrapping his arm around me. "If you've changed your mind, it's okay. We don't have to go. We can go back inside."

Even though he doesn't complain, I'm sure Miguel is tired of being cooped up inside so much. It's not fair to him. And I know more often than not, he chooses to stay in with me.

"No, I haven't changed my mind. It's just hard."

He leans down and kisses the top of my head. "I know."

"I want to do this, Miguel. I really do."

"How about we just walk to the elevator? We'll stop there and think it over. How's that?"

I smile. "Baby steps." It's all about those baby steps.

"That's right." He takes my hand and gently pulls me forward.

I take one step, then another. And another. And before I know it, we're at the elevator.

"So, what do you think?" he asks.

I find myself staring at the call button. At that down arrow. "What if there's someone on the elevator?"

"If there is, we'll wait for the next one."

I nod. "Okay."

"Do you want to push the button, or should I?"

"I'll do it." My hand shakes, but I manage to press the button. Immediately, the elevator doors open, revealing an empty car.

"It's all ours," he says. He holds out his arm to brace the doors open.

I stare into the elevator as my pulse races. My heart's pounding, and my chest feels tight.

"Together," he says, and he gently pulls me by the hand into the car. Once we're in, he pushes the button for the ground floor.

When the doors whoosh shut, I stumble backward

until my back meets the wall.

Still, he's right beside me. "You're doing great," he whispers, and then he drops a light kiss on my lips.

I know what comes next. We've talked through this a dozen times. The elevator will let us out in the ground floor lobby. We'll cross the wide-open space and exit from the front revolving doors. We'll walk across the parking lot to the sidewalk, and then it's a two-block walk to Lake Shore Drive. We'll cross at the crosswalk, and then it's just a few hundred yards to the beach.

The beach.

Lake Michigan.

And people. Lots of people.

The elevator does a little shimmy when we reach the lobby. Fortunately, we didn't have to stop for any other passengers. The doors slide open, and Miguel guides me out. It's Saturday morning, and the lobby is bustling with people coming and going from the building.

"To the doors," he murmurs, reminding me.

I nod.

The guards at the front desk smile and nod to us as we pass by. As we make our way to the revolving doors, other residents come into the building laden with shopping bags. They're all smiling, their faces flushed. A few of them smile politely as they pass us, having no idea that I'm *this close* to having a meltdown and escaping back upstairs to our apartment.

But I don't want to make a scene, and I don't want to embarrass Miguel.

A moment later, I realize we're standing still in the center of the lobby, while a small crowd passes us. A woman with a baby in a stroller walks past us. A young couple with a small dog on a leash are next.

Miguel's hand slowly runs up and down my back, a warm, comforting reminder that he's here with me.

The two things I've wanted for so long are right in front of me—security and a normal life. I just have to have the courage to reach for them. Miguel gives me the security I need, but the normalcy part is up to me.

I take another step forward, toward the doors. Miguel keeps pace with me. A boisterous group of teenage boys races into the building, talking loudly, jostling each other. One of them is holding a basketball, which he tosses to a friend. The friend has to scramble to catch it, bringing him right into our path. Their friends howl with laughter.

"Hey, guys," Miguel says to them as he steers me out of harm's way. "Take it down a notch, okay?"

"Yeah, man, sorry," says the boy holding the basketball.

They continue on their way, laughing and elbowing each other.

Another few steps brings us to the revolving doors. Miguel holds me right in front of himself and we step through together. We're deposited outside the building near the valet parking podium. Cars are lined up in front of the building, along with taxis.

Miguel steers me to the side, and we head for the sidewalk. When we reach the walk, he turns me to face him and peers down at me. "Doing okay?"

I nod, but I must look far from okay because Miguel frowns.

"Are you sure?" he asks.

"I'm sure."

It's two blocks to Lake Shore Drive.

Just two blocks.

I can do this.

As we pass townhouse after townhouse, I squeeze Miguel's hand. The sidewalk is relatively empty at the moment, but I can hear the boisterous crowd on the beach—children's laughter, squeals of delight, dogs barking.

As we approach Lake Shore Drive, the sound of traffic is nearly deafening. So many lanes of traffic streaming by. Every time I hear a car horn, I flinch. While we wait at the crosswalk for the light to change, a small crowd gathers around us—families, couples, people on bikes, people on skates, joggers. Miguel pulls me close, his arm around me. I'm pressed against his body, which is a reminder that I'm not alone. He's with me. He'll keep me safe.

This is real life. This is the real world, and I'm standing in the middle of it. I'm part of it, just like everyone around me. I glance up at Miguel and find him watching me intently. He smiles, and I smile back.

I can do this.

33

Miguel

When we cross Lake Shore Drive and head down the walk to the beach, I'm elated for Ruby's sake. I honestly wasn't sure we'd make it this far. There were a few times along the way that her anxiety seemed to take hold of her, and she'd stop in her tracks. But each time, she'd resume walking, and now here we are. We're standing on the beach.

Ruby kicks off her sandals and grabs them by their straps and holds them in her free hand. I have a death grip on her other hand, just as a precaution. I'm prepared for absolutely anything.

I look down as she buries her toes in the sand. She's smiling, and when she glances up at me, I see tears glittering in her eyes.

"I'm here," she says in awe. "I'm really here. I did it."

"Yes, you did." I kiss her.

We hear the bell from the cart of Mexican popsicles.

"How about a popsicle?" I ask her.

She spots the man pushing the cart of popsicles and smiles. "Oh, my God, there he is! Come on!"

We catch up with the vendor, and I order two popsicles. Ruby unwraps hers—Tropical Medley—tastes it, and sighs. "It's just as I remembered."

We walk barefoot along the beach, the water splashing over our feet, holding hands and enjoying our popsicles. Ruby seems a bit tense—she flinches at loud noises—but overall she's doing well. I think—I hope—that this is the first step of many more to come. My goal, my dream for her, is to make it possible for her to enjoy a normal life, go out and do things. Have fun.

We finish our popsicles and toss the sticks into a trash can. We're at the far end of the beach now, where very few people are. It's quiet here, and Ruby seems more relaxed.

When we come across a bench beneath the shade of a massive oak tree, we sit together. I put my arm around her, and she leans into me.

"So, what do you think?" I ask her.

"It's better than I imagined."

"Would you like to do this again?"

She nods. "Yes, definitely."

I kiss her temple. "I'm proud of you."

She gazes up at me. "I couldn't have done this without you." She turns to sit facing me and reaches for my hand, linking our fingers together. "Thank you, for being you. For giving me the sense of safety I so badly needed. Between you and Edward, I feel like I've been given a new lease on life. Like I get a second chance." She cups my face and runs her thumb across my lips. "Would you be terribly surprised if I said I love you?"

My heart stops, skipping a full beat, before it starts racing. "Surprised? Yes. But also terribly glad to hear it." I chuckle. "I think I fell in love with you the moment I first saw you, but I never in a million years dreamed you could feel the same way. You reminded me of a beautiful princess trapped in a tower, but I knew I was hardly prince material."

"That's where you're wrong, Miguel Rodriguez. You are definitely prince material." And then she rises up in her seat and kisses me. She takes one of my hands in hers and presses it to her chest. "You're my prince."

I thread my fingers in her hair and bring her in for another kiss. I drag her closer, and she straddles my lap, facing me as we kiss. Fortunately, there's no one else close enough to get an eyeful.

Finally, she pulls back, her cheeks flushed, her blue eyes sparkling. "Miguel Rodriquez, would you be mine forever?"

I nod, stunned by her request. I tuck a loose strand of her hair behind her ear. "Only if you'll be mine forever, too."

She smiles. "I'd love to."

Epilogue

Three months later
Ruby

Tonight's not the first time I'll be leaving the apartment, but it's definitely the most nerve-racking excursion for me so far. Since our first trip to the beach, we've gone to the lake every weekend to walk around and get a Mexican popsicle. I've been to Layla's apartment quite a few times to hang out with her, usually when Miguel had to go somewhere. Or she comes over to visit me. I've even been to visit Miguel's grandmother, who is an absolute doll. She started crying when I gave her the little portrait I painted of Sugar, her tiny Chihuahua. I think she's officially taken me under her wing.

But tonight's different. Tonight is *scary*.

"We don't have to go," Miguel says for the third time today. "Don't feel like you have to say yes, because I'm okay with missing it."

Miguel and his friends have had this long-standing Friday night meet-up at a bar called Tanks, but since he started protecting me, he's missed quite a few of these get-togethers. I feel bad that he's been missing out on this tradition, but he insists it's okay. That he doesn't mind. But I mind. I mind being the reason he's missing out on something that means a lot to him.

So tonight we're going. It's going to be crowded and noisy. There will be drinking, music, dancing, pool, and darts.

Lots of noise.

Lots of people.

I'm a nervous wreck. I feel queasy.

Right now I'm in the bathroom brushing my hair and putting on a bit of mascara and lip gloss.

"You look beautiful," Miguel says. He's leaning against the bathroom doorjamb looking edible in a pair of black jeans and a black T-shirt. He's literally the epitome of tall, dark, and handsome.

"So do you," I say, grinning.

Miguel gets flustered when I tell him he's beautiful.

He comes into the room and stands behind me, a full head taller than I am. I barely come up to his chin. When I stand beside him, I feel almost petite. My flaming red hair contrasts with his midnight black hair. I think we make a striking couple.

He gathers my hair in his hands and smiles when I shiver at the delicious electricity streaking down my spine. "We don't have to go," he says, leaning down to whisper in my ear. His breath ruffles my hair, and I shiver again. "I mean it. We can stay home tonight and watch a movie."

I meet his gaze in the mirror. "You don't think I can do this?"

He looks thoughtful, because he's honest, which is one of the many things I love about this man. He's honest, and he doesn't bullshit me. "I think it's going to be hard for you. It's going to be loud and crowded. You haven't been around that many people in such a small space in a really long time."

I sigh. "I can do this."

His hands slip around my waist, and he leans down

to kiss my cheek. "Rome wasn't built in a day, you know. Baby steps, remember?"

"Layla's going to be there, as well as Charlie and Erin. I'll be fine. Plus, I'll have you. I'm not worried."

He presses his lips against the back of my head. "Liar."

"Okay, yes, I'm worried, but I want to do this. I don't want you to keep missing out on things you like to do because of me. I don't want to hold you back."

"Sweetheart." He turns me and lifts me up to sit on the counter. Then he steps between my knees. "You are my number one priority." He drops a kiss on my nose. "Everything else is secondary, including hanging out with my friends."

I reach up to cup his handsome face and stare deep into those obsidian eyes. "I want to do this, Miguel. I want to *try*."

He frowns. "Fine. But if it gets to be too much, I want you to tell me. We'll come right home, okay?"

"Deal."

He holds out his little finger. "Pinky swear."

I grin and hook my little finger around his. "I swear."

"All right. Let's go."

As we head for the door, I stop to give Pumpkin a scratch. "Don't worry. We won't be out late."

Miguel grabs his key fob and wallet. I grab my purse. We meet up by the door.

As I stand there watching Miguel unlock the deadbolt and release the chain, my pulse speeds up and I find it harder to breathe.

Here we go.

After he slides the chain lock free, he grasps the door knob and looks down at me. "Ready?"

I grab hold of his waistband and nod.

Miguel opens the door slowly and peers out into the hallway. "It's empty. We'll walk to the elevator, take it down to the parking garage, then walk to my car. Okay?"

"I nod. Okay."

Miguel steps out into the hallway and holds out his hand. I lay mine in his, and he links our fingers. I stand in place for a good minute, trying to drum up the courage to step through the doorway. He stands there quietly, patiently, not rushing me. He never rushes me.

I glance left and right and left again. The hallway's empty.

Miguel squeezes my hand. "I won't let anything happen to you. I promise."

I nod. Intellectually, I know he won't. But emotionally, it's not so easy. I do feel better knowing he's armed beneath his black leather jacket. If someone attacks us, we won't be helpless.

I place one foot across the threshold, then the other. While I stand there acclimating to the idea of being outside our apartment, Miguel locks up behind me.

"Ready?" he asks. He slips his free arm around me and pulls me close. "Anytime you want to call this off, just say so."

I square my shoulders. "It's okay. I'm doing this." I want Miguel to spend time with his friends, doing the things they like to do. I don't want to be the one who holds him back, who limits what he can and can't do.

I want a *normal* life.

We walk slowly down the hallway to the elevator. Miguel reaches out and pushes the down button. The doors open to reveal two young women dressed to go out for the evening. They're young, about my age. One blonde, and one with dark hair. I don't miss their reactions when they get a look at Miguel.

Miguel glances down at me. "Ready?"

I step into the elevator, and he follows me. The doors close behind us, and we turn to face them, leaving the other two girls behind us. I hear them whispering, and one of them snickers quietly. I imagine they're crushing on Miguel.

Miguel presses the button for the parking garage. The elevator car descends smoothly. We don't talk. He just tightens his grip on my hand and holds me against him.

The doors open in the main lobby, and the two girls step around us and exit the car. The blonde glances back at Miguel and gives him a blatant come-hither smile. I want to smack her.

Miguel chuckles as the elevator doors close once more, and we continue down to the garage.

The next time the doors open, we're in the parking garage. At the sight of the expansive, rather dark space— the lines of parked cars—it sends my pulse pounding.

A parking garage. Why does it have to be a parking garage?

"I'm sorry. I wasn't thinking," Miguel says. "I should have moved the car to a spot closer to the elevator."

"No, this is okay. I have to get used to parking garages."

When I nod to him, Miguel steps out into the cool parking garage. I follow him. When the elevator doors behind us close, I flinch.

"It's okay," he says. He nods to our right. "I'm parked over there." He points to a long row of parked cars. "It's not that far."

I'm shaking, but he doesn't say anything. We walk in silence. I'm hypervigilant, my gaze scanning the rows of cars, looking for someone threatening. Being in this garage is bringing back so many bad memories. Mentally, I shake myself and try to focus on the positive. We're going to see our friends. This is a big step for me—I'm out and about, doing normal couples things.

Miguel tightens his hold on me. "Take a deep breath." He demonstrates, taking a slow and deep breath, then letting it out. He nods just ahead of us. "Here we are."

I stand shaking while Miguel opens the front passenger door. I slide into the seat, staring straight ahead. I grip the seat with both hands while he grabs the seatbelt and pulls it across me. He's crouching next to me, looking me in the eye. "You're doing great."

I nod, but don't say anything. I don't trust myself to speak. If I do, I might burst into tears, and I don't want to do that.

Miguel stands and closes my door. He walks around the back of the car to the driver's side and slides behind the wheel. A moment later, we're backing out of the parking spot.

I sit perfectly still, a death grip on my seat, and close my eyes until we're out of the garage.

Once we're on the road, I lean my head back in my seat and try to control my breathing. The last thing I need is to have a panic attack. If I did, I know Miguel would turn around and take me back to the apartment. I don't want to be that girl. I don't want to be a liability for him.

It's a twenty-minute drive through Friday evening traffic. When I feel the car come to a stop, I open my eyes and see that we're parked along the curb under a large tree. It's still light outside. We're parked in front of a thrift shop with vintage clothes and purses displayed in the shop windows.

Miguel shuts off the engine and walks around to open my door. I have to force myself to release my grip on my seat so I can step out of the vehicle.

We're in a commercial district filled with shops and restaurants, so the sidewalks are crowded. The traffic is bumper to bumper, moving slowly.

Miguel puts his arm around me and steers me straight ahead. "It's just two blocks," he says.

We walk arm in arm to the bar. There's a bit of a line forming at the door, so we have to wait a few minutes to get inside.

It's loud in the bar as TVs compete with a jukebox and people conversing. It's somewhat dark in here, not quite what I expected.

Miguel leads me to a long table where I spot several familiar faces—Layla and Jason, of course. And Charlie. Philip—I remember him from the time he came to my old apartment to install a security system. I recognize Liam McIntyre from the YouTube videos we watched one evening of him fighting in a boxing ring. His girlfriend, Jasmine, is here. And another couple I've met before—Erin and Mack.

Layla stands and gives me a hug. Charlie scoots out of the booth and hugs me as well.

Layla had saved two seats next to her. I take the one right beside her, and Miguel sits on my other side.

Once I'm seated, Layla hands us menus.

Miguel puts an arm across my shoulder and leans in close. "Doing okay?"

I nod. "Fine. I'm fine." But the truth is, my heart is pounding. I glance around the wide-open space at a huge crowd of people. Some are seated, eating and drinking and talking. Others are on the dance floor. Some are playing pool. Every seat at the bar is taken, and behind the bar are at least four staff members scurrying all over the place to serve their customers.

So many people. It's overwhelming.

I feel so open and exposed. So vulnerable.

Miguel reaches for my hand under the table. He strokes the back of my hand, the movement calm and comforting. His lips brush my hair. "Everything's fine," he says quietly. He squeezes my hand and chuckles. "You're sitting at a table filled with professional bodyguards. Trust me when I say you couldn't be in safer hands."

I manage a smile and nod.

We order food and drinks. And while we're waiting for our food to arrive, one of the couples—Liam and Jasmine—go out onto the dance floor.

Our drinks come. Miguel and I both ordered Cokes. As I take a sip of my cold drink, my pulse continues to race. When my chest tightens, I take a deep breath.

Layla leans toward me and says, "Ruby, I'm so proud of you."

I look her way and find her smiling at me.

"You did it," she says. "You're here."

Earlier in the week, I told her we might come tonight, but that I wasn't absolutely sure. I promised I'd try, though. When she raises her glass of water in my direction, I raise my glass, and we toast.

I feel anxiety's grip on my chest loosen a little bit, and I can breathe better.

I notice Miguel watching us with a satisfied grin on his face. He leans close and kisses my temple. "I'm proud of you, too."

And suddenly, I find myself smiling. *I did it! I'm here.* It's a small step, sure, but it's a huge step for me. Hopefully one of many more to come.

Our food arrives, and we eat. When we're done, Miguel asks our server for our check.

"Ready to go?" he asks me after he's paid our bill.

I nod, relieved. "Yes, I'm ready."

Layla hugs me goodbye, as does Charlie.

It's just starting to get dark out when we walk hand-in-hand back to Miguel's car.

"How are you feeling?" he asks.

"Terrified." I laugh. "But also proud of myself. I did it."

He pulls me close and slips his arm around me. "Yes, you did. When you feel up for a really big challenge, we can join my family for a Sunday dinner. You can meet my family, my grandparents, and lots of aunts, uncles, and cousins."

"Oh, my." That does sound like a challenge.

When we reach the Mustang, Miguel opens the door for me, and I slide into the car. On the drive back to our building, I'm mesmerized by the streetlights and the strings of fairy lights hanging in front of storefronts. "I forgot how pretty downtown Chicago is at night."

"You think this is pretty?" Miguel asks. "Let's drive down North Michigan Avenue, past the bridge, so you can see the restaurants along The Chicago River. That's really a sight."

"Okay."

He looks at me in surprise. "Really? You want to?"

"Sure, let's do it."

Miguel chuckles. "Next thing you know, you'll let me take you to Navy Pier."

"I remember Mom and Edward taking me to Navy Pier once when I was little. I think I'd like that. Maybe we can take Edward with us."

Miguel reaches for my hand. "I think that's a fantastic idea."

When we arrive back at our building, Miguel parks near the elevators in the underground garage. He whisks me out of the car, sweeping me up into his arms, and carries me to the elevator. I squeal out of a mixture of embarrassment and amusement.

When the elevator doors open, a small crowd of teenagers emerges, all of them staring at us.

Miguel carries me into the elevator, and when the

doors close, leaving us alone, he kisses me breathless.

The elevator lets us out on our floor, and Miguel continues carrying me.

I laugh. "Put me down, silly. I can walk."

He sets me on my feet outside our door and fishes in his pocket for his keys. "How does it feel to be home?" he asks as he opens our door.

"Wonderful," I say as I step inside.

Pumpkin runs up to greet us, and I bend down to pet him.

This is our home now. After discussing it, Miguel and I have decided we want to stay here permanently. I love the view of the lake, but more importantly, I love being close to our friends. Layla and I, especially, have become quite close. We're constantly running back and forth between each other's apartment.

* * *

That night, as we're lying in Miguel's bed—we've started sleeping in his bed as it's bigger than mine—with Pumpkin curled up at our feet, Miguel reaches into the top drawer of his nightstand and retrieves a small black velvet jewelry box. He opens it, revealing a slender gold band set with a gorgeous, sparkling red ruby. "I realize this might be too soon," he says.

I'm sure my eyes are as wide as saucers when I shake my head. "It's not."

He smiles. "I love you more each day, and I don't ever want to live a single day without you." When my eyes tear up, he kisses me gently. "I'll be your knight, your protector, for the rest of your life if you'll have me."

My throat tightens, and I think this can't possibly be happening. "You know how I am. Are you sure?"

"Yes, I know you, and I love all of you," he says. "I'm sure."

Pumpkin chooses that moment to walk across me to get between us. He head-butts Miguel's hand that holds the ring box.

"It's a package deal," I say. "If you want me, you get Pumpkin, too."

He chuckles. "I accept." He takes the ring from the box and slips it onto my ring finger on my left hand. He kisses me, and then he says, *"Eres mi vida para siempre."*

His voice and the words are lovely. "What does that mean?"

"It means, 'You are my life forever.'"

* * *

Thank you for reading *Freeing Ruby*. I hope you enjoyed Ruby and Miguel's story. Stay tuned for more books in the *McIntyre Security Protectors* series.

* * *

If you'd like to receive free bonus content each month—exclusive for my newsletter subscribers—sign up for my newsletter on my website. You can also find links to my free short stories, information on upcoming releases, a reading order, and more.
www.aprilwilsonauthor.com

* * *

Here are links to my list of audiobooks:
www.aprilwilsonauthor.com/audiobooks

* * *

I interact daily with readers in my Facebook reader group (April Wilson Reader Group) where I post frequent updates and share teasers. Come join me!

Books by April Wilson

McIntyre Security Bodyguard Series:

Vulnerable

Fearless

Shane–a novella

Broken

Shattered

Imperfect

Ruined

Hostage

Redeemed

Marry Me–a novella

Snowbound–a novella

Regret

With This Ring–a novella

Collateral Damage

Special Delivery

Vanished

McIntyre Security Bodyguard Series Box Sets:

Box Set 1

Box Set 2

Box Set 3

Box Set 4

McIntyre Security Protectors:
Finding Layla
Damaged Goods
Freeing Ruby

McIntyre Search and Rescue:
Search and Rescue
Lost and Found
Tattered and Torn

Tyler Jamison Novels:
Somebody to Love
Somebody to Hold
Somebody to Cherish

A British Billionaire Romance Series:
Charmed
Captivated

Miscellaneous Books:
Falling for His Bodyguard

* * *

Audiobooks by April Wilson
For links to my audiobooks, please visit my website:
www.aprilwilsonauthor.com/audiobooks

Made in the USA
Columbia, SC
28 October 2023